"Chocolate mousse, and now this," Halley murmured happily.

"Which is better?" Nick asked, dropping little kisses along her neck.

"Hard to say. They're both sinfully delicious."

The heat from his kisses inflamed her, and every tiny part of her was sparked to life. "Nick . . ."

"Yes, my love?"

"My contact lens fell out. I think it might be on me somewhere."

"Halley, you say the most romantic things. Here, let me look." With sure fingers, Nick explored the front of her dress, brushing his hands across the silk that covered her hips, then sliding upward toward the low scooped neckline. "Don't see it here," he said huskily.

His movements were turning her mind to mush. Halley took a quick breath, and Nick responded immediately. "Maybe in the front there," he suggested, reaching just inside the bodice to rub the lacy edge of her camisole with his fingers. "Nope, can't seem to find that contact."

"You've found plenty of contact, Nick. I can't breathe. Stop, please."

He made one last caressing search, then held the delicate lens in his palm.

"I won't ask when you found it," she murmured, giving him a mischievous smile.

"Good idea," Nick agreed. "But if it gets lost again, at least I'll know the territory."

WHAT ARE *LOVESWEPT* ROMANCES?

They are stories of true romance and touching emotion. We believe those two very important ingredients are constants in our highly sensual and very believable stories in the *LOVESWEPT* line. Our goal is to give you, the reader, stories of consistently high quality that may sometimes make you laugh, sometimes make you cry, but are always fresh and creative and contain many delightful surprises within their pages.

Most romance fans read an enormous number of books. Those they truly love, they keep. Others may be traded with friends and soon forgotten. We hope that each *LOVESWEPT* romance will be a treasure—a "keeper." We will always try to publish

LOVE STORIES YOU'LL NEVER FORGET
BY AUTHORS YOU'LL ALWAYS REMEMBER

The Editors

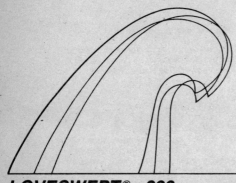

LOVESWEPT® • 233

Sally Goldenbaum
The Baron

BANTAM BOOKS
TORONTO • NEW YORK • LONDON • SYDNEY • AUCKLAND

THE BARON

A Bantam Book / January 1988

Published simultaneously in the United States and Canada

Bantam Books are published by Bantam Books, Inc. Its trade-
mark, consisting of the words "Bantam Books" and the por-
trayal of a rooster, is Registered in U.S. Patent and Trademark
Office and in other countries. Marca Registrada. Bantam
Books, Inc., 666 Fifth Avenue, New York, New York 10103.

PRINTED IN THE UNITED STATES OF AMERICA

O   0 9 8 7 6 5 4 3 2 1

One

Halley Finnegan raised one white-gloved hand to her carefully made-up lips. Her large emerald green eyes grew larger as she leaned through the open car window and stared at the elaborate house she was about to enter.

"Good grief," she said, choking. "I'll need a tour guide just to get me through the weekend!"

Reluctantly she opened the door of her tiny Volkswagen and got out. She teetered sideways almost instantly, her slender body weaving like a reed in a high wind. Grasping the door handle for support, Halley stared down accusingly at the unfamiliar spike heels. She'd never make it inside in them. She grimaced as she scanned the crimson dress that hugged her hips like a girdle and squeezed her pale, full breasts so tightly that she felt sure a sneeze would leave her naked. It had to have been Rosie's cheap wine. Nothing else could possibly have made her agree that the dress was perfect for the occasion!

The thought of Rosie Wilson brought a smile to her face. Rosie had delighted in rummaging through every shelf and dusty box in her antique clothing shop the previous night to outfit Halley for the weekend, and the venture had ended in hilarious laughter as the two friends finally settled on the sexy crimson dress and filmy shawl that did little to cover Halley's skin.

"Finnegan, it's the chance of a lifetime!" Rose had insisted, her dramatic flair with words making the ridiculous sound sensible. "A whirlwind weekend of mystery and charade! And the more exotic you look, the more you'll melt into the crowd. If you try to dress like Halley Finnegan, you'll stand out like a sore thumb!"

It was only after the second glass of wine that Halley had tried on the dress. It was after a third glass that she had agreed to wear it. Rose had stared at her lean, lovely curves with envy. "I'd look like a fortune-teller in that, Finn. But you look positively regal. No one will ever guess you're a fill-in houseguest!"

Houseguest. The thought jolted her attention back to the magnificent house that stretched out before her. The mansion sat atop a gentle rise like a jeweled crown, its opulence and grandeur borrowed from another time. Off in the distance, beyond the rolling lawns, Halley could see a shimmering lake, its surface streaked in shadow by the setting sun. She didn't hear any violins yet, but the graceful strains of Mozart and Beethoven fit the scene so perfectly, she fully expected to tune in to them at any moment. It was the perfect setting for a Fitzgerald novel, Halley mused as she cautiously approached the wide fan of marble steps leading up to the entrance. Or a romance. Or a murder.

The last thought sent an uncomfortable ripple of apprehension through her body. That was, after all, why she was there. She shivered, drawing the lacy shawl up over her bare shoulders, and walked slowly up the steps.

Why, oh, why had she let Leo Thorne talk her into

coming, anyway? She'd give almost anything to be somewhere else, preferably curled up in her favorite library chair, burying herself in a wonderful musty book! But when her kindly benefactor had asked her to go as a favor to him, he had left her no room for a refusal. His dear, dear friends were hosting this charming party—a murder-mystery weekend, plotted and directed by a professional troupe—and all the guests would participate.

"Such a clever idea, Halley, eh?" His grin had been barely visible beneath his bushy white mustache. The problem was, he'd explained, that one guest had come down with the flu at the last minute and he didn't think Halley would mind filling in. Furthermore, he had insisted it would actually be a wonderful thing for her to get away from the Thorne Estate Library for a brief vacation. *A fortuitous change of pace. Refreshing. Invigorating.*

Halley had stared at him wide-eyed, assuming he'd been nipping from the bottle he kept on a bookshelf behind the fat, leather volume of *Banking Strategies.* Luck wasn't on her side, however. Mr. Thorne had been dead serious.

There was no way on God's earth she could turn the man down. Aside from her family, he had done more for Halley Finnegan than any other human alive, and when she reluctantly agreed, the spread of happy wrinkles around his eyes *almost* made having to go to the party worth it.

Until now. Halley wet her lips nervously and glanced back toward the circular drive, her gaze settling on the tiny green Volkswagen. It looked pathetic in the grandiose surroundings. "Don't worry, my green knight," she whispered softly. "If I can do it, so can you. . . ."

With a feeble burst of energy Halley Finnegan spun around to face her first—and *last*, pray to God! —murder-mystery party.

She paused on the top step. She could hear voices coming from around the side of the house and through the open windows. The happy clink of ice against fine glass mingled with laughing chatter. She hadn't missed the cocktails, after all. So much for *that* effort!

She eyed the shiny brass door knocker with renewed determination and smoothed her palms down over the flaming red dress. *Well, Finnegan, here goes.* With a forced bravado that painted a crimson blush across her high cheekbones, Halley lifted the knocker and let it drop firmly against the heavy oak door.

In seconds the door opened wide and a gray-haired butler filled the opening. His gaze met hers, then fell almost immediately to her dress. Halley felt a rush of damp heat travel up her neck, then back down to the cleavage the elderly man eyed so admiringly.

"Ah," he managed, pulling his gaze upward and wiping away the tiny beads of perspiration that dotted his forehead, "welcome, madam. Please, won't you come in?" He backed up stiffly against the door to let Halley pass.

Halley paused, her heart hammering beneath her ribs. There was still time to feign a polite excuse and leave, to hurry back to the warm security of the Thorne Estate, to slip into her familiar warm-up clothes and tennies and sink her teeth into any one of a million projects she was halfway through. She could . . . No, of course she couldn't. Besides, she decided with a sudden grin and a lift of her head that brought the doting butler to full attention, she was anonymous, playing a part. Rosie was absolutely right! She could be whoever she wanted to be. It was the only way to get through the crazy weekend, and she'd do it come hell or high water.

A tingle of childlike pleasure eased through Halley, pushing the nervousness aside, as she began to look at the situation as a challenge. When it came right down to the wire, she'd always been able to tap into her ever-ready reservoir of strength and make the most of it. Wasn't that what Joe Finnegan had always taught his kids to do?

With head held high and her thick auburn hair cascading down the bare, creamy skin of her back, Halley Finnegan whisked gracefully past the butler, then turned and faced him with a smile so alluring, it caused the elderly gentleman to cough behind his hand.

"Please, sir," Halley said huskily, "kindly tell the Harringtons that the Contessa Ambrosia is here."

At that moment a tiny silver-haired lady appeared from the other side of a giant fern, her bright oval eyes sparkling and a flowing Grecian gown trailing behind her.

"My dear, welcome!" She grasped Halley's hand and looked up into her face, smiling. "I am Sylvia Harrington. And you *must* be dear Leo's friend. He's told us so very much about you, and I cannot tell you how grateful we are that you agreed to come at the last minute like this!" Her small head bounced along with the words. "Now, tell me, just to remind me, of course"— she touched her cheek lightly with one finger, a small crease lining her still smooth brow—"you are . . . ?"

Halley smiled. "Halley. Halley Fin—"

The woman reached up and covered Halley's mouth with her small gloved hand. "Shh! No, no, no, dear. We won't use any of *those* names this weekend. No, no. This weekend you are . . ." She reached over and picked up a small scroll lying on the side table in the formal entrance hall. "Ah, here! You are the Contessa Ambrosia, of course." She stepped back and looked Halley over from head to toe. A *perfect* contessa, I should say. My, oh, my." Her eyes traveled over the silk gown. "What a lovely, lovely dress, my dear. You are ravishing!"

Halley smiled back and felt the fantasy taking shape around her. Her hostess, dressed as an Italian princess, was lovely, and her own dress hadn't been condemned—not yet, anyway—and she—plain Halley Finnegan—was a contessa.

"Ravishing, indeed!" The deep, husky voice that swept into the conversation was disembodied at first, and Halley delighted in the resonance of it. It was a marvelous voice, the kind one would sit back and enjoy from the last row of a theater as it rolled off the stage in huge waves.

"And who *is* this ravishing creature?"

The owner of the voice took her hand and swept her gloved fingers to his warm lips, which kissed her fingers through the thin material and left hot imprints on her skin.

"This," Mrs. Harrington said graciously and with a great deal of enthusiasm, "is our final guest. The Contessa Ambrosia." She curled her arm around Halley's waist.

"And this, Contessa, is Baron von Bluster." Sylvia Harrington giggled at the fictitious name. "Goodness, Nick, how perfect a name for you!" She tweaked his cheek affectionately.

Halley raised her head slowly, her thick lashes lifting until she looked directly into the Baron's eyes— soft black eyes that nearly swallowed her.

A smile spread across his darkly handsome face. Halley shivered. She opened her mouth to speak, but her hostess gushed on in warm, silvery tones. "And such a happy chance that you should have walked in, my dear Baron, because the lovely Contessa happens to be your partner for the weekend. Ah, such a good match; I shall have to commend my dear Herbert on his farsightedness." She chuckled happily, patted Halley's shoulder, then swept off, leaving Halley and the Baron facing each other in the middle of the spacious hallway.

Halley realized with a start that the tall, tuxedoed stranger still held her hand. She slipped it from between his fingers and crossed her arms delicately over her chest.

The Baron's husky laughter echoed in the marble chamber. "Ah, already I've learned something about the beautiful Contessa. She isn't accustomed to wearing such daring—albeit beautiful—attire."

Halley dropped her arms immediately and tilted her chin up. "Not really, Baron. A slight draft, that's all."

He nodded, but his eyes reflected warm laughter. "Good. Come, then, and we'll find a cocktail to ward off the chill." He circled her waist with one arm and guided her through the hallway and toward a set of French doors.

Halley hadn't bargained on this at all. She'd anticipated the tedious cocktail chatter and having to mingle with strangers, but she hadn't anticipated, not for one blessed instant, having her own baron for the entire weekend. The thought was humorous and utterly terrifying at once. Halley wet her lips and hurried to match his long, loose stride. *Please, God,* she begged, *let's emphasize the humor here!*

The man beside her was calm and collected and probably had never known a second of terror in his life. Halley sighed silently.

"Now, tell me, beautiful lady," the Baron's deep voice whispered softly into her hair, shattering her thoughts, "what else is the enchanting Contessa not accustomed to, so I may help put you at ease?"

She glanced up into his smoky eyes and noticed the slight brush of gray at his temples. Put her at ease? She lifted one hand to her cheek and smiled coyly. "Absolutely nothing, Baron."

"Nothing?"

His gaze was hungry now, and Halley swallowed hard around the lump in her throat, keeping her smile firmly in place, her chin tilted upward, and her gaze locked tightly to his. She wasn't Halley Finnegan, she was the Contessa, she reminded herself. It was all a crazy game. "Nothing of consequence, Baron."

"Good! Then let's move on to cocktails. Oh, and I suppose we ought to squeeze in falling in love."

Halley stumbled over the edge of the carpet and grasped his arm for support. "Falling in love, you say?"

His fingers moved playfully on her waist as he spoke. "Didn't you read your invitation, Contessa?" His smile was charming and teasing and sexy.

"Seems I missed something. Was it in the small print, perhaps?"

"Exactly. There it was, right after the date and place. 'The Baron von Bluster and Contessa Ambrosia,' it read, 'are both recovering from wild affairs and are thrown together after a separation of many years. In spite of the suspicion and suspense wrought by the murder, they find the old flames rekindled, and love blossoms in the shadow of murder and intrigue.' " The Baron cleared his throat dramatically, causing Halley to laugh softly as he continued. " 'But when the Baron admits he is bankrupt and stands to inherit millions from the deceased, tension builds.' "

"It said that?" Halley's brows narrowed suspiciously.

He held up one hand and grinned. "Scout's honor. That's who we are. The token lovebirds—"

A contessa . . . a baron . . . and now a wild affair? It was too much for Halley. Bubbly laughter welled up inside her chest. If she had tried to imagine a life as far removed as possible from her plain, comfortable job at the Thorne Estate Library, this would fit the bill perfectly!

"So, lovely Contessa," he went on, holding open the French doors, "as you can plainly see, we have much ground to cover!"

"All those years apart." Halley shook her head.

"Yes, I've been damn lonely, my dear!"

"But the wild affairs, sir? Certainly the nights weren't *too* lonely."

"Wild only in a mechanical way, Contessa. Nothing could compare to the pure passion we shared!"

Their light laughter mingled as they walked over to the far edge of the stone patio and looked out onto the breathtaking panorama before them. The fiery ball of sun was settling on the far edge of the lake, seemingly held up only by the clear line of the horizon. Below, the rippling waters caught the fading light, and centered perfectly, as if by an invisible artist, a lone sailboat glided across the magnificent vista.

"What a beautiful sight!" Halley pressed her palms flat against the cool surface of the stone wall edging the terrace.

The Baron edged up close beside her and rested one hip against the rough wall. "It's a wonderful place. Why Syl and Herb ever venture off the property is beyond me."

"Are they good friends of yours?"

He nodded. "Yes, and more so. They're relatives— Aunt Sylvia and Uncle Herbert." He rescued two glasses of champagne from a passing waiter's tray as he spoke. "And they coerce me into many of their gatherings. I think they consider my being unmarried a devastatingly lonely existence. But tell me, Contessa, how did you happen upon this soiree? I don't believe I've seen you here before."

Halley smiled. "No, you haven't. I'm here by default, actually. One guest couldn't make it, and a dear old friend of mine plugged me into the vacancy as a favor to the Harringtons. Apparently the mystery weekend needed all the characters to be a success."

The Baron lightly tapped his glass against hers and flashed her a charming smile. "Well, it certainly needed you! Here's to the Contessa-by-default. Long may she live."

Halley sipped the champagne, then smiled broadly. "How appropriate a toast! What does one do if one *doesn't* live long at a murder-mystery party?"

The Baron's answering smile held a hint of a dimple in one cheek. "Oh, the important people—like you, my Contessa—will survive. The victim will be one of the acting troupe mingling so subtly among us. But, fair lady"—his thick brows drew together ominously—"we're all *suspects*."

"Aha!" Halley took another sip of the champagne. "So I'm cavorting with a would-be, could-be murderer?"

"But what does it all matter?" He moved closer to her. "We've found each other again, dear Contessa, and *that's* all that matters." His husky laughter hung in the warm evening air.

Halley rubbed her hands up and down her bare arms to ward off a shiver.

"Still cold?" One thick brow lifted in concern.

Halley shook her head quickly. "I'm fine, thanks."

The Baron watched her closely, his eyes lingering on the rise of her breasts.

She recognized the look that played briefly across his face. What would he do when he discovered with whom he'd been saddled? Not a sophisticated jet-setter at all, not even a sophisticated lady of the night, as her friend Leo so delicately put it, but a librarian who ranked formal parties right below measles on her list of things to avoid! She hid her laughter behind a quick question. "Tell me, Baron, besides falling in love, what is expected of us tonight?"

"You can handle more? Well, dinner, I believe, and meeting and mingling, music and laughter, that sort of thing."

"And the murder?"

"Ah! I've probably got a real life P.I. on my hands. . . ."

He lifted one brow questioningly, and Halley tossed her head. "Not even close, Baron."

He watched her intently and tried to read beneath the incredible emerald color of her eyes. More emerald, that was all he found. A deep, wonderful sea of it. But there was *something* different—enchantingly different—about the Contessa, he realized. The Baron smiled, then edged even closer. "All right, I'll tell you about the murder." He whispered the words conspiratorially into her ear. "The victim is out there somewhere. And the dastardly perpetrator of the crime is too. And the clues are everywhere—"

"I suppose we ought to see about finding them—"

The Baron grinned and stood tall beside her. "Yes, and I'm being terribly unfair to keep you all to myself like this. Syl will have my hide; she wanted me to introduce you around to the other guests in this little drama. I guess I'll have to share you." He took her hand and tucked it inside the crook of his arm. "But only for a while. After all, we have all those lost years to catch up on, my lovely Tessa."

My lovely Tessa . . . Halley basked in the fantasy of it all for a second, then smoothly swept across the room on his arm, her eyes lustrous and her head held high.

As they approached each group, Halley noticed the admiring looks, the questioning brows that indicated the people were wondering who she *really* was, but the Baron introduced her only as the Contessa, and before long, Halley began to feel as if her slippers were made of glass and her pumpkin were waiting just outside the door. She had a *long* time to go before midnight.

Dinner was a whirlwind of animated conversation and rich food served at round, linen-draped tables. Dozens of servants hovered over the guests, and a string quartet played on a small balcony off the dining room.

There were twenty-four guests in all, and Halley marveled at how eagerly each one of them fell into his or her role. There was a proper spinster, a fading movie star, and, of course, a butler among the guests, and near her at her table sat a Mafia don in black tie, chewing a fat cigar. Kids playing dress-up and finding unexpected delight in being someone else, she mused. Just as she was doing.

Her glance swept around the elegant table for the twentieth time that night and paused as it had each time on the profile of the magnificent Baron, sitting directly to her left. It would have been hard not to look at him, so imposing a presence was he. Halley Finnegan's Baron—for two days. The thought sent unexpected chills up and down her spine. Who was he really, beneath the elegant tux and lovely talk? He fit the role of baron so perfectly, it was difficult to think of him as anyone else. Most of the guests had greeted him warmly and familiarly, some slipping and calling him Nick. Nick the Baron, with the laughing, dark eyes and the splash of gray at his temples. He was laughing now at something the older woman on his left had said, and Halley watched him over the rim of her wineglass.

A deep, bellowing voice interrupted her thoughts. Herb Harrington leaned toward her, the buttons of his four-star general's costume straining against his chest. "Ah, the Contessa is enjoying herself. Good!"

Halley pushed her thoughts to the back of her mind and nodded to her host. "Leo Thorne was right on target, Mr. Harrington. Your parties *are* unusual! This is the nicest group of could-be murderers I've mingled with in some time."

He laughed heartily and patted her hand. "Well, Syl and I like a good time, Contessa. Yes, we do. And the Baron, is he introducing you to people?"

"Oh, yes. Baron von Bluster certainly seems to know his way around."

"Ah, so I see his reputation can't stay under wraps, even under that baronial title."

Halley shook her head quickly. "Oh, no, I only meant *here*. Everyone . . . well, he seems to know all the guests." She glanced at Nick, but he was busy talking to someone.

"Oh, that he does! Yes, ma'am, the Baron knows everyone, right, Abbie?" Herb smiled at an elderly woman with clear brown eyes who was sitting to his right.

Halley had noticed her earlier with a distinguished-looking man who had thinning gray hair, and whom Halley assumed was the woman's husband. They seemed to take special note of her when Nick had introduced them on the patio. She searched her memory for names, and when they came to her, she realized they weren't using their real names, anyway. She knew them only as the once famous vaudeville team of Otto and Olive Bailey.

The woman smiled warmly at Halley. "Yes, the Baron does know many people. And you seem to be getting along well, Contessa. So the Baron is being good to you?"

Halley smiled. "Oh, he's being very patient with me. I'm new at all this, you see. I—" She suddenly felt embarrassed. The woman was watching her so closely. It was not an unkind look, though, but rather one of intense interest.

"Well, young lady, I can see in our Nick's eyes that *he's* enjoying himself. That's good." She nodded her head carefully and thoughtfully.

Herb rested one hand over the woman's and spoke kindly. "You see, Abbie? Who knows . . ." His voice drifted off then as he turned to summon a waiter for dessert, and the older woman's attention was taken by the gentleman seated next to her.

Halley pondered over the strange conversation for a moment, then realized she simply wasn't used to dinner party chatter, that's all. *And* barons.

A gentle pressure on her leg beneath the drape of the tablecloth scattered her thoughts. For a fraction of a second she thought it was a dog, until a soft, very human whisper caressed her ear. "You've been giving far too much of your attention away to others, Contessa."

Halley jumped slightly. "Baron, you scared me! Is that you playing games with my knee beneath the table?"

"Hmm, perhaps we should both go down to check?"

"Wouldn't that be a perfect moment for the murder? No, Baron, I don't think it's a wise move."

He nodded in mock seriousness. "You're right, of course. We'll save that until later. For now, though—" he cupped her free hand in his and pressed it to his lips—"we can simply relax in the pure delight of being together." His kiss lingered on her fingers long after she had rescued her hand and slipped it down into her lap.

A gravelly voice from across the table broke in. "Ho, Baron von Bluster, you have found yourself a lovely woman there, I see!"

Nick looked over at the Mafia Don and chuckled. He was really an Episcopalian minister and was obviously enjoying his role immensely. "Well, sir, the way I see it, we need to make this party a success. And the only way is to play our parts to the hilt."

The plump man lifted his glass in wholehearted agreement, then swallowed its contents in a single gulp. "Right you are, Nick. Eat, play games, and be merry, for tomorrow you may die!" He laughed at his own joke, and Halley found herself joining in. He was having so much fun playing his role that it was contagious.

"So, lovely lady, who are you?" The Don sat back and patted his wide girth.

"This, Don Siciliano," Nick said, "is the exquisite Contessa Ambrosia, named for the gods' nectar and every bit as sweet." Nick leaned sideways and kissed Halley gently on the cheek.

"Aha, the Contessa! How lovely you look. And how lovely for you and the Baron to have found each other again. Lovers should be together." He chuckled merrily, then added with a wink, "You see, I read my invitation carefully."

Halley felt Nick's fingers once again doing tap dances on her knee. The silky material of her dress slid back and forth beneath his fingers, and she wondered how soon it would be before her labored breathing would cause her breasts to spill out of the form-fitting gown.

"Yes," the elderly female vaudeville star chimed in from Halley's right, not seeming to notice her plight. "I agree, Don Siciliano. It's about time Nick—ah, the Baron, excuse me—found a love."

Nick smiled at the woman, and Halley noticed it was a softer, more intimate smile than he offered to the others. The Baron cared a great deal for Olive Bailey, whoever she was.

Halley managed a smile about the time Nick's fingers began a slow massage. Fighting him was simply too tiring, she realized as she bit down painfully hard on her bottom lip. And there was no need to, anyway. It was all a game . . . and no one had ever accused Halley of being a poor sport! Playing along was the only practical course of action.

"Yes, and being apart has been dastardly!" Halley announced with gushing enthusiasm. She wound her arm through Nick's and pressed her cheek against his smooth tux, her face tilted up to smile at him with sensuous longing.

Nick grinned down at her and fingered a lock of silky hair. The evening was getting better and better, he decided. "Remember the last time we met?"

"In Antibes, wasn't it, darling?" Halley asked, fluttering her eyelashes. Antibes—where *was* Antibes, anyway?

"Hell, why couldn't *I* have been cast as a baron?" the butler complained. "Care to trade, sir?"

"Not on your life! It's about time I got lucky." Nick wrapped his arm around the back of her chair, and his fingers pressed lightly on the bare flesh of her upper arm. "And my Tessa here is about the most beautiful good-luck charm a man could hope for."

His look invited a response, and Halley smiled a sophisticated, sexy, contessalike smile at him that surprised even herself.

A shuffling of chairs and the ringing of a tiny silver bell by Herb Harrington quieted the guests, and Herb rose from his seat.

"Welcome, friends," he said in deep Shakespearean tones. "By now you have probably all met, but I'd like to introduce you one more time, just in case you may have missed one or two of our treasured guests. Take careful note as I do"—his voice plunged ominously—"because right here among us we have someone who will no longer be here on the morrow, and another who is responsible for his or her demise."

A ripple of laughter swept through the room, then Herb went on, introducing each guest and following up the introduction with a humorous note about the character.

Halley was introduced right after a Russian Czar, and she managed to keep her smile bright and level, even during Herb's declaration that she "and the Baron could certainly be using their reconciliation as a front to plot something far more dangerous." Nothing, she knew with clear certainty, could be more dangerous than a "reconciliation" with the mysterious Baron.

"And now," Herb continued, his eyes sparkling brightly, "the party will continue outdoors with music and dancing and boat rides. As you mingle, you are to keep your ears and eyes open to hints and clues. And once the crime is committed, no matchbook cover should go unchecked, no torn business card overlooked, no strange packages left unopened. And . . . no guest should be overlooked as a possible suspect."

Animated chatter once again filled the room, and Herb quieted them for one final directive. "The party will end with a buffet tomorrow evening, at which time all of you will demonstrate your deft powers of deduction and attempt to point the finger of accusation in the right direction. A prize—marvelous, of course—will be awarded our supersleuth. Meal schedules and such are in each of your suites, and the staff is available for anything you might need. Go now"—his large hands swept the air—"and mingle, my friends. With . . . murder!"

The room was filled instantly with excited conversation and the shuffling of chairs as people got up from their tables.

Nick whispered into Halley's ear, "What will it be, my Tessa? Dancing? A boat ride? Or perhaps we could retire to my guest suite and renew old acquaintances?"

"Oh, I hardly think we'd find clues in your suite. Much too obvious!" Halley's words tumbled out on top of each other, her mind racing. Even the Contessa wasn't ready to tackle that last choice! And although she'd love to dance, her feet were beginning to feel like bruised cucumbers in Rosie's skinny heels; she knew she wouldn't last on the dance floor. "How about a short walk?"

Nick's warm smile was her answer, and they walked outside and down the cobbled path that cut through the rolling lawns as it wound its way to the lakeshore. Halley breathed in the crisp night air. So this was what Cinderella had gone through. Lovely . . .

"What are you thinking?" The Baron's deep voice matched her dreamlike mood, and she smiled.

"That I've had enough champagne tonight to last me the rest of the year. That the meal was absolutely fantastic. That it's a lovely, beautiful night and that I'm enjoying myself."

"You forgot one thing."

"Oh?" She tilted her head sideways.

"You forgot to mention that the Contessa is surprised at her enjoyment."

"Well, sure, a little surprised. I did have other plans for the weekend—"

"Oh? Let me guess." His arm slipped around her waist as they walked, his brows drawing together in an expression of exaggerated concentration. "You were planning on spending it in the solitude of a great museum, admiring magnificent works of art."

She shook her head and smiled.

"No? Well, then, let me try again." His free hand swept the air in front of them. "I have it! You were to be the guest of honor at a gala charity dinner for the preservation of pigeons, a lavish event attended by the rich and famous."

Halley laughed as she loosened herself from his hold and slipped down a side path and onto a curved bench that was surrounded by a cluster of bushes. A circle of thick-growing cedar trees backed the foliage and formed a grove, lit only by the moonlight trickling through the branches.

"Please, may we sit for a second? I find your conjectures delightful, but my feet are absolutely killing me." She slipped off the shoes and sighed deeply. "Oh, that feels wonderful! I've been wanting to get out of those high heels all night."

Nick sat down beside her and watched the slow graceful movement of her legs as she stretched them out before her. "Here, let me."

Before Halley could respond, he bent over and lifted both her feet, sliding them across his knees while her whole body rotated automatically on the cool stone. "I know just the trick," he said calmly. With both of her stockinged feet in his lap, he slowly began to massage the tender arches.

Halley's eyes widened and her mouth dropped open, but there wasn't time to refuse. She clasped the bench tightly on either side of her. "You . . . you're a masseur back there in the real world, right?" Her voice sounded choppy, reaching her ears in starts and stops. But Nick's fingers gently rubbing and pushing into her tired feet felt magnificent, and she closed her eyes and let her head drop back on her shoulders. "Hmmm, that feels absolutely wonderful. Even if it turns out you *are* the murderer."

His answering laugh filled the dark cove. "Contessa, you surprise me." Nick watched her face closely as he spoke. "Here we are in our own private grotto, just the two of us. Aren't you afraid?"

"Certainly not. Why would I be afraid?" Because he might seduce her? No, no one, most especially a handsome baron, would seduce a quiet librarian with freckles on her chest. Didn't he know that? A small smile teased up the corners of her lips.

"Good." His palms enclosed her ankles, and he rotated his hands gently, trying to ease the tiredness out of her bones. "I'm not afraid of you, either, although contessas, I'm told, are born to passion and are often quite aggressive."

Halley held her face up to catch the breeze and cool the hot blush that swept across her cheeks. His hands, on her ankles, were doing surprising things to her heartbeat as well as to other parts of her body. She took a quick breath and sought a contessa-like answer.

"Yes, Baron," she finally said, smiling at him down the length of her nose as the power of the masquerade rescued her. "But we're also taught the fine art of control. And, dear Baron, I've mastered it beautifully." There, she'd handled that well—well enough to make her wonder briefly if perhaps she had been royalty in another life.

The Baron sneaked his fingers beneath the hem of the slinky red dress and crawled them slowly over the smooth, firm skin of her legs. Her dress collected around the stiff white cuffs of his shirt and rode up along with his movements.

"Hey!" Halley shot up, her eyes wide as her body reacted violently to his explorations.

Nick grinned slowly. "Perfect control, hmm?"

"Baron," she demanded feverishly, "remove your hands from beneath my dress immediately."

Nick Harrington wasn't at all used to listening to the pleas of ladies in situations like this because the women usually meant the opposite of what they said. But then, the freckled Contessa was not like anyone Nick had ever met before. He removed his hands and smiled softly. "Sorry, just wanted to know the extent of that control. You're a pretty sensuous lady, you know."

"You're speaking in non sequiturs, Baron. A definite breach of logic." She swung her bare feet down to the ground and wiggled her toes.

Nick threw his head back and laughed. "Tessa, I think I'm falling in love."

"Well, good," Halley said as primly and calmly as she could manage, her palms pushing away the wrinkles on her dress. "You're following the script nicely, Nick."

"Nick? Now how did he get in here? It's not fair, you know, that you know my name and I know absolutely nothing about you." He sidled closer to her.

She lifted her chin slightly. "Fair? There was nothing on *my* invitation, dear Baron, that said a thing about being fair. Now come." She stood and looked down at him in the purple shadows. "Let's head back. All this fantasy has made me terribly tired. I think it's time I hit the hay."

Nick watched her as she rose from the bench. A stray beam of moonlight splashed across her face and lit her remarkably honest green eyes. More women than he could count had said the same thing to him in the past four years—in slightly different words, of course, but she was probably the first one who meant she wanted to go to bed . . . alone . . . to sleep.

His smile went unnoticed by Halley, who was feeling around the pebbled walkway with her toes in an effort to find the spike-heeled shoes. Beneath that wonderful makeup job and sexy dress, Nick decided thoughtfully, was someone who had never come within fifty miles of a contessa in her life.

"Here, contessa, allow me." He bent over and picked up her shoes, slipping each one onto an arched foot while she balanced herself with one hand on his back.

"Thank you. I feel like Cinderella."

"In that case, you'd have to leave one shoe behind, and those pebbles would hurt like hell."

Halley nodded. "Right." She comfortably hooked one arm through his. "I'd also have to run off, and there's no way on earth I'd be able to manage that tonight."

"Good." He looked down and smiled softly. "I don't want you running off." He led her carefully back toward the well-lit terrace of the Harrington estate.

Later that night Halley stood barefoot before the French doors of her bedroom. Outside, all was still, except for the gentle breath of a breeze through the giant maple trees and several couples who strolled across the broad expanse of lawn. Tiny gaslights dotted the blackness like fireflies. Halley breathed deeply, then slipped through the doors and out onto the tiny, private patio, shielded from view by a thick, circular hedge of yew bushes and clumps of mulberry.

"A real fantasyland," she murmured as the breeze ruffled her filmy nightgown.

She thought of her own apartment, a world away on the other side of Philadelphia. It was a cluttered, homey space in the old gatekeeper's cottage on the Thorne Estate where she worked. Then she looked back through the open doors into the perfectly lit suite to which she'd been assigned for the weekend. *Everything* was perfect. The glistening white-silk and chrome furniture was accented by a slight smattering of pastel colors here and there on the upholstery and wall coverings.

She tried to imagine all her friends and acquaintances here, in this setting. It was hard to visualize. The Thorne Estate had been donated to the community by the Thorne family, and Halley loved her job there as director of the library, which was located in the main house. She loved the tiny cottage that was open to her friends at all hours of the day and night. She thought of them flopping on her couch and ordering pizza, laughing and crying and feeling completely at home. She thought of Archie, the hobo who lived behind the library in the old stable and sometimes came for tea in the gazebo, and the neighborhood kids who pasted their rubbings from the old cemetery grave markers on her walls.

Halley burst out laughing. No, these were *definitely* two different worlds.

But she *could* picture Nick, the Baron, here. Sure, she could see him easily stretched out on that long, lovely couch in his handsome tuxedo. Even when the wind had ruffled his dark hair as they walked along the path earlier, it hadn't looked mussed. Nothing about him was haphazard, not his long, lean physique, nor his way of conversing, nor his elegant mannerisms. The Baron von Bluster was definitely not haphazard. But what *was* he, exactly?

Halley looked up into the sliver of a moon that caught her eye and whispered, "A dashing, romantic dream. That's what the Baron is."

A piercing scream from out of the darkness shattered her thoughts into a million tiny pieces.

Immediately following was a shot and a bellow and a scuffling of footsteps, although later Halley wouldn't be able to tell anyone in what exact order these events had occurred.

She stood frozen in place, the hair on her arms and back of her neck standing upright.

And then, in seconds, impulse took over, and without a backward glance she plowed through the carefully manicured yew bushes and ran down toward the lake and the sound, her gown flattening against her body in the breeze.

Two

A crowd had already gathered near the edge of the lake when Halley, breathless and disheveled, arrived. "What is it?" She said, panting. "I heard a scream!"

Herb Harrington stood nearby in an elegantly tailored smoking jacket, every gray hair in place and a finely carved pipe held comfortably between his fingers. He looked over at Halley with a pleased smile. "I do believe we have a crime on our hands."

Halley looked more closely into the circle of people. A male figure was prone on the tiny strip of beach that bordered the lake, his head resting sideways on the sand. Halley recognized the dramatic flash of white hair and the aquiline nose as belonging to one of the guests she had met earlier.

"A . . . a . . . of course, a murder!" Realization swept over her, along with a rush of embarrassment. "Oh, Lord, I thought . . . I really thought—" She began to shiver as the adrenaline slowed and the night breeze chilled her arms. When she peered closer at the man, she noticed a slight rising and falling of his chest and caught the small smile that flickered across his lips just a moment before uniformed men lifted him onto a stretcher. Halley grinned back at him, convinced he had gotten the best part to play. At least he got to sleep.

The deep, husky words that tickled her neck came from directly behind her. "And where were you, miss, at approximately 12:02 A.M.?" Nick's broad hands covered her bare shoulders.

Halley turned around slowly.

Nick was still dressed in his tuxedo, but the jacket was flung over one shoulder now, and the stiff, white shirt sleeves were rolled partway up his forearms. The dark thatches of hair on each arm contrasted with the moonlit white of his shirt.

She smiled. "I definitely wasn't cut out for the life of a contessa, Baron, nor this life of murder and mayhem. I almost called the police. For real!"

Nick laughed. "Well, it was a bit eerie, the scream and shot and all." He took her hand and pulled her slightly away while actors dressed as policemen edged their way through the crowd of guests. A small, mustached man talking like the famed Hercule Poirot seemed to be in charge.

"It's too bad this crime wasn't planned for the Orient Express," Halley said as she watched the questioning of the guests. "That's always been a secret dream of mine."

"Well, then, if that's a secret dream of yours, we'll do it," Nick said.

She chuckled. "Of course. And my glass slippers will be waiting in Istanbul."

"And anything else your heart desires."

Halley felt his gaze lower to her heart and was suddenly aware of the scant clothing that only partially covered her. She quickly crossed her arms over the filmy lace that stretched across her breasts.

"Cold?" Nick smiled.

Halley wet her bottom lip. She felt silly and embarrassed, standing in the moonlight in her nightgown. And she felt cold. *Freezing*, in fact.

"Yes." Her fingers wrapped around her upper arms. "I think I'll head back."

"Before being questioned?" Nick touched the back of her neck and lifted his fingers into her hair. One thick brow lifted in reprimand. "Contessa, you may end up in jail!"

Halley tossed her head and smiled at him. "At least I won't have pneumonia! 'Night, Baron."

She turned and strode off into the night.

Nick followed. Several long strides brought him to her side. "I don't think you should walk back alone. Not with a murderer on the loose," he murmured.

Halley looked at him out of the corner of her eye and said, teasing, "How do I know I'm safe with you? Do *you* have an alibi for 12:02?"

"Well, I, ah—" He appeared confused.

Halley looked at him more closely, and the expression on his face answered her question. The Baron *did* have an alibi, and she was most probably curvaceous and lovely—one of the gorgeous lady guests who had showered such lavish attention on him earlier. She nodded knowingly and ignored the strange sense of discomfort she felt, then changed the subject quickly. "Nick, may I borrow your jacket?"

With a quick, smooth gesture he draped it over her bare shoulders. "Sorry, Contessa. I wasn't thinking." It wasn't entirely true that he hadn't been thinking. No, he'd been thinking a great deal about those bare shoulders . . . about the expanses of lovely, creamy skin that glistened in the moonlight and the pale, sensuous mounds visible beneath the web of fine lace. In fact, he'd thought a great deal about all parts of Contessa Ambrosia for several hours now. He looked down into the thick, silky mass of hair. "Better?"

"Much. Thanks."

"To where are we fleeing?"

"I'm not sure about you, Baron, but I'm pooped

and am heading for bed. I'm usually out like a light by eleven."

"What an ordered life you must lead."

Her laugh was husky. "Hardly! Although people have *tried* to impose some semblance of order on me for almost twenty-seven years now."

Nick dropped one hand lightly onto her shoulder. "So you're the spontaneous, impulsive sort."

She looked up into his eyes. "No. Just disorganized. But I work well that way and manage to get things done. Give me a neat, orderly desk and I fall apart."

Nick fingered a wayward slip of hair that had fallen across his hand. He was trying very hard to picture his lovely Tessa's leading a disarrayed life. At a desk. Without the carefully applied makeup. Without those clothes . . .

"Here we are, Nick."

Halley stopped walking when she reached the slight break in the bushes through which she had pushed herself earlier. She paused, then smiled up into Nick's thoughtful gaze. "Well, good night."

"May I come in?"

"Why?" The single, ungracious word jumped out, and Halley wished she could quickly grab it back. "I mean, it's late, Nick. You must be tired, and we have a whole day of partying yet to go tomorrow. Conserve the resources, you know." She laughed and slipped from beneath the warm, musky-smelling jacket. "Here's your jacket, and thank you."

Nick took it and stood there for a second, watching as Halley turned and pressed through the bushes. She was almost across the small flagstone patio when he separated the bushes farther and followed.

Halley spun around. "You're persistent, aren't you?"

Her voice was calm, but Nick caught the slight edge of irritation. "Wait, Contessa. Just a few minutes, please?"

His tone was gentle and friendly, and his eyes still flashed from dark depths, still held that sensuous sparkle. They also held something else, something Halley couldn't quite put her finger on. Then it dawned on her: The Baron, for a brief second in the shadowy light of the moon, looked lonely.

Halley rubbed her cheek, then looked back into her suite. When she turned to Nick again, her face was lit by a smile.

"Okay, but only for a few minutes. I really do need sleep."

Nick reached beyond her and opened the door. The boyishness melted away beneath his husky voice. "Certainly not for beauty."

A bright blue knit cardigan was lying across one of the chairs, and Halley quickly moved toward it and slipped her arms through the sleeves. What was all this about, anyway? One minute he looked like he needed a sisterly hug and a chocolate malt; the next he was coming on to her and telling her—plain-Jane Halley Finnegan—that she was beautiful. Wouldn't her romantic friend Rosie love it all!

"No, not for beauty, Baron." She scooped up some books and a pair of glasses from the couch and dropped them onto the coffee table so Nick could sit down. "I don't worry about that. Life is far too short."

Nick watched her unaffected, casual movements as she slipped out of her slippers and sat down beside him. She curled her feet up beneath her and pulled the thick sweater down until it nearly covered the entire flimsy negligee. She was so damned unspoiled. And so sexy in an incredibly unpretentious way. His very own barefoot contessa. A delighted grin softened his face.

Halley's brows lifted. "Now, Baron, was there something in particular you wanted to talk about?"

Nick hadn't the faintest idea why he had insisted on coming in. Oh, he knew what he'd *like*, but he'd known, too, there was no way in hell he'd end up in bed tonight with the Contessa. Still, there was something there besides those fires she'd lit in him, and he couldn't seem to let her go, to walk away from whatever that something was. "As a matter of fact, there is something else, Tessa."

Halley leaned her head to one side, waiting.

"I . . . I find you intriguing." Hell, he felt like a kid on a first date! His wide mouth curved into a lop-sided grin. "As a matter of fact, I like you very much, Contessa-whoever-you-are."

Halley rubbed her cheek thoughtfully with two fingers, a habit her friend Rosie teased her about. Watch out, she'd say with a laugh, Finnegan's brain patterns are going berserk again! It wasn't actually her brain patterns going berserk this time, it was her heart . . . and other parts of her. And on top of it all was the incredible urge to laugh at the whole crazy, irrational, extraordinary scene.

The laugh mellowed into a smile, and Halley's gaze finally met the black eyes that hadn't stopped staring at her face. "Good. Intriguing is something I've never quite carried off before. Perhaps I've gotten something from this weekend, after all."

"You don't like weekend parties?"

"It depends."

"On?" Nick had moved several inches closer to her on the couch.

Halley wondered why breathing had suddenly become complicated. "This is fine, as parties go." She wanted to smile and laugh and tell him about late-night pizza parties on the floor of her living room, and picnics following the library fund-raisers. *Her* kind of parties. But she couldn't seem to say another word.

"Contessa, I'm deadly serious."

Halley forced a laugh. "Oh, dear, *deadly* isn't a word to throw around lightly here."

Nick touched her lightly on the shoulder. "You're safe with me," he murmured.

Oh, dear, no. If this was safe, what was *dangerous* in this man's world? Halley swallowed hard.

"I meant what I said before, Tessa. You're lovely and different, and I hope we can make the most of this weekend."

"Stop it!" Halley's face was so close to his, she could feel his breath on her cheeks and her heart beat wildly. "I think the fantasy element of this weekend has gone to your head, Baron."

"It's not my *head* I'm worried about."

"You don't even know who I am or what I do. I could be a lady of the streets, an actress hired by the mystery troupe . . . a . . . a . . ." She was breathing hard now and wasn't even aware that her sweater had fallen open and her nearly naked breasts were almost touching his body.

"I don't give a damn what you do, but I'm absolutely intrigued by who you are. I'd like to know lots more about you, Tessa. Find out what books you read and what you like in your coffee—"

"I don't drink coffee," Halley said quickly.

He moved closer. "I want to learn why you blush when I flirt with you, then appear so damn competent and sure of yourself when you pull away."

"I *am* competent. The competent contessa, that's me," Halley whispered. The chill that had been in the air earlier had long disappeared, and she felt a thin beading of perspiration collecting between her breasts. She was sure the lights were dimming, as his hand settled lightly on her leg.

"I . . . love . . . competence . . ." he said as his lips closed over hers with gentle, sure pressure.

"Hmm," she answered as her eyelashes swept down and she gave in to the warm surge of delight that eased through her body. She opened her eyes halfway.

"I'm still here," he murmured in the tiny space between them.

"I thought so," she said.

Nick's eyes were wide open, caressing her face. He touched her cheek with one finger, running it lightly across her lips and up over the delicate cheekbones. How could one kiss bring him to the brink like this? He felt the pressure building and squeezed his eyes shut.

Halley waited, but instead of the warm press of his lips, a cold draft of air swept across her face. Her eyes shot wide open.

Nick was lifting himself off the couch, his long legs firm in front of her. He turned and leaned over, one arm straddling each side of her, his hands brushing her thighs as they pressed into the couch.

Halley dared to look up at him.

Nick dipped his head and kissed the end of her nose. If he didn't get out that door in one minute, he wouldn't be able to account for his actions, and what it would mean to the Contessa tomorrow. For reasons his foggy mind couldn't come to grips with right now, Nick cared about tomorrow. "It's late."

Halley nodded mutely.

"And you're tired."

"Oh, very," Halley answered in a voice that didn't sound like her own.

Nick laughed as if she had said something funny, and dipped his head lower until a shock of his black hair fell forward and touched her face. He rotated his head gently, his smooth skin sliding across her heated forehead. Then he dropped tiny kisses across her cheeks and stretched back up to his full height. "I even love your freckles, Tessa. Now get a good night's sleep. I'll see you in the morning."

He was gone in a flash of black-and-white tuxedo, and in his wake was a vast ocean of heat.

• • •

"Contessa!" Nick strode across the library from where he'd stood next to the carved fireplace. A dozen heads turned and watched him, their gazes settling with obvious enjoyment on the figure in the doorway.

Halley stood still, waiting for him to reach her side. Protection, that's what she needed, although she was not for one minute going to admit that Rosie's choice for the Contessa's "day outfit" embarrassed her silly. It was the kind of outfit one saw in *Vogue* and laughed at, knowing no one—absolutely *no one*—but 110-pound models ever wore such things. The black ultrasuede skirt was just above her knees and fit to perfection, and the dips and plunges of the pure silk emerald blouse were definitely designed by a *man*, one with a fertile imagination. Halley fingered the filmy scarf that was tied Isadora Duncan–style around her neck. She lifted her chin and held her contessa smile carefully in place. "Good morning, Baron."

She nodded amicably to the other guests seated on couches and Queen Anne chairs in the sun-splashed room. Her gaze finally settled on the Don's friendly face. "You're looking quite dapper this morning, Don Siciliano."

The aging minister rose as if drawn by a magnet. "Thank you, Contessa. I'm feeling absolutely marvelous! Well, as marvelous as one can feel when immersed in a dreadful murder investigation!"

Halley chuckled and let Nick lead her over to an empty love seat where they sat down side by side. A servant appeared as if by magic and offered coffee, tea, and crumpets.

"The Contessa doesn't drink coffee. Tea, please." Nick's attention drew knowing smiles from those nearby.

Halley shot him a look. "You have a fine memory."

He winked and shifted his body until his thigh

pressed closely against the ultrasuede of her skirt. "But it was only last night, darling . . ."

Eyebrows lifted, and Halley vowed to keep her cheeks a pale rose rather than the bright scarlet that was threatening to color her whole body. "Yes . . ." she murmured, calling upon the role of Contessa to help her through. "Ah, last night—" she said, and then turned to the guest-butler who hovered over the sofa, capturing any bit of attention Halley was willing to throw his way.

But there was no way on earth she could blot out the heat of Nick's body next to hers, nor was Nick about to let her forget he was there. "Be careful what you say to him. I think he did it," he whispered carefully into her hair as she tried to talk calmly with the butler.

"Why?" Halley turned slightly toward him, wondering what would happen if she sighed aloud in the elegant parlor.

"It's the ears. One can always tell by the ears," he said, his voice laced with seductive laughter.

Halley nodded slowly, as if she had actually absorbed what he'd said rather than the searing rays created by his fingers on her thigh.

Just then the Hercule Poirot look-alike entered the room, and everyone hushed in giddy anticipation.

"The murder weapon has been found!" he announced jubilantly. "Mr. Lucius A. March has been killed with a large knitting needle, one sharp stick— clean, quick, and oh, so deadly."

Nick's hand moved to the rhythm of the actor's words, tapping out the course of the crime on her leg the whole time the detective questioned the guests. He outlined a ray of sunlight that landed conveniently on her thigh, and whispered sensuous comments about their supposed rendezvous in Antibes.

By the time the detective got around to questioning Halley and Nick, Nick's arm was around her shoulders, the color in her cheeks was brilliant, and the detective commented in a charming French accent on the incredible eroticism of young lovers sitting in sunlight. Halley groaned.

Lunch was a brief respite, served on glass-topped tables out on the terrace, thanks to the Indian summer weather. The guest-butler had finally managed to get seated next to Halley and wasn't about to let Nick edge his way in. "Sorry, Baron, but she's mine for lunch. *All* mine."

Halley took full advantage of the cooling-off period, breathing in the fresh air and filling her mind with thoughts other than of the Baron's hands on her body.

But her break was short-lived.

After the raspberry meringue dessert and champagne, Herb announced that the next several hours could be spent looking for clues. The guests were on their own until six o'clock, when they'd all gather on the terrace and make their final assessment of the crime.

"I have a hunch," Nick whispered close to her ear.

Halley was standing near the edge of the terrace, watching one of the maids wander down to the dock. "You do?" she asked.

"Follow me."

He led her down a path that led to a wooded area bordering the lake.

"Shh," he cautioned with one finger to his lips as they walked stealthily along the tree-rooted path.

Halley followed directly behind him, her eyes tracing the firm ridges of muscles beneath his forest-green polo shirt. He hadn't dressed as carefully in character today as she had, but then, how was she to know what barons wore when sleuthing? She laughed softly into the fragrant air. Her head felt light from champagne and fantasy, and her skin was warm from the sunlight falling through the branches.

The lake curled around to their right, and on the other side the woods thickened, pathways spreading out in several directions. "What should I be looking for?" Halley asked softly, wishing she'd been able to change into jeans and tennis shoes.

"Snakes," Nick whispered back. "The place is full of them."

"Nick!" She flew into his back, her arms wrapping around his waist.

"You called?" He turned slowly, his arms slipping around her and pulling her close to his chest.

"I . . . I like bugs and most animals, but I have this thing about reptiles." Her voice was a frightened whisper. "And my legs are . . . so bare!"

Nick looked down at the stretch of firm, creamy skin. Yes, they were. So were her shoulders, *and* a goodly portion of her chest. And every inch of her smelled lovely, a clean, soapy smell that was far more heady than the champagne they'd had at lunch. "Don't worry, Tessa. I'm here." His words were murmured, and he held her close.

"Is—is there perhaps a snakeless place we could look for clues?" she asked, her voice still shaky.

"There's a little cottage ahead that's sometimes used for guests. There, see?" He pointed through some trees, and Halley noticed a small clearing right on the edge of the lake.

"That looks like it should be packed full of clues." Halley nudged Nick toward it and followed close behind.

They stepped together into the well-mowed clearing, and Halley breathed a sigh of relief. "Well, Baron, now you know my vulnerable spot."

Nick looked her over carefully, and she discovered his eyes had the same effect on her that his hands had. "That's it? That's your only vulnerable area?"

She blushed. "Yep. That's it. Other than a fear of snakes, I'm made of iron." There was no reason to be as close to Nick as she was, but no matter how hard her mind tried, her body refused to pull away. His touch was so gentle, and all the sensations that raced through her and glued her to the spot were mesmerizing and wonderful.

"Oh, now, my Contessa, there you're dead wrong. What I'm feeling isn't cold iron at all; it's warm and quite grand." Nick's hands moved up and down her arms. They had walked as far as the low steps that led up to the vine-covered cottage, and Halley bumped the back of her leg against the bottom step.

"Clues?" she murmured from somewhere in the back of her throat.

"Ah, yes, clues. They must be here somewhere," Nick agreed, his gaze searching her face. "I'm sure we can find some." His hands slipped from her shoulders down to the center of her back. He pulled her close.

The searing warmth of Nick's body electrified her. She tried to get her mind to work, but nothing registered. Her lips parted, and his slanted down over them in delicious possession. He kissed her hungrily this time, his excitement fueled by her own.

It had to be the clothes, Halley thought wildly. They were somehow drugging her, making her act like someone else. But deep down inside she knew The surging desire she felt for the Baron belonged to no one but Halley Finnegan. Then she allowed the kiss to deepen, her body delighting in the taste of him.

"Seems," a hearty voice said, "that everyone thought the old guest house was the place to head for clues."

Halley instinctively jerked away, and Nick was left standing apart from her, a brilliant green scarf dangling from his fingers. They looked up into the dancing eyes of the guest who had been playing the part of a fading actress.

She was standing in the doorway of the cottage, just in front of the man dressed as the butler. "We didn't mean to interrupt," her tone was apologetic, "in fact, we were just leaving."

Nick chuckled and took a step that brought him back up beside Halley. "Joanna, I should have known you'd head this way."

Halley marveled at Nick's composure, his deep voice teasing the woman nicely, his expression friendly and calm. She couldn't have spoken if her life depended on it. Halley had never been kissed quite like that before—or at least she'd never experienced such resounding aftershocks. Her legs were wobbly, her lips felt deliciously bruised, and she was sure every freckle on her nose was dotted with perspiration.

Nick slipped an arm around her waist, and they stepped aside as Joanna and the guest-butler walked down the steps.

"Well," Nick asked as they walked by, "have you two solved the mystery?"

"Actually we haven't a clue," Joanna said, smiling enigmatically.

"Well, then," Halley said, finally finding her voice, "I guess we might as well not waste our time here."

"Oh, Contessa," Joanna said pleasantly, nudging Nick at the same time, "I wouldn't call it a waste of time at all!"

"Nor I," Nick agreed, and slipped his fingers up beneath the thick fall of Halley's hair.

"Nevertheless," Halley said more calmly, her chin rising in contessalike confidence, "perhaps if we all explore together, we'll have better luck." The words hung falsely in the air, but she tried to follow them up with a dazzling smile. The thought of that empty cottage and the unbridled desire racing crazily through her body was more than she could handle right now. Casual tumbles weren't her style at all, but Nick—the Baron—was exerting a power over her she knew she couldn't fight.

Nick's head was angled to one side, and he looked at her carefully. The weekend was definitely turning into more of a mystery than was promised on the invitation, he decided. He slipped an arm around her waist and started toward the path. His voice was a husky whisper. "Whatever you say, Contessa, but we have hours to go before we slip off into the real world. . . ."

The half hour before cocktails was a "rest period," as Sylvia had called it, a time for people to think through their clues, ready their bags for departure, and freshen up before the buffet dinner.

Halley spent it pacing the length of the patio. The few clues they had gathered—some cotton yarn found beside the path and a piece of black nylon stocking caught on a bush—went unheeded as thoughts of Nick filled her head.

They had wandered through the rest of the afternoon as acutely aware of each other as if they had stayed on in the deserted cottage. Nick touched Halley constantly, and she marveled at the power of those touches. A palm placed flat on her lower back, a curved finger along her cheek, his hip brushing against hers—each was enough to send waves of warmth rushing through her until she felt no part of her was left untouched.

No, the identity of the murderer wasn't the real mystery here. The *real* mystery was how in the world she was going to get through the final hours intact.

"And what do you want to keep intact, Finnegan?" she asked herself with a grimace.

"Everything! My fine, sterling reputation as a

woman who is wise and cautious in the ways of love."

"Which is why you never have any fun!" chided a voice in her head that sounded curiously like Rosie's.

"Fun, *schmun!* I've had a *grand* time." Yes, of course she had, and there was no need to worry. She took a deep breath and walked back into the suite. "No need to worry," she repeated aloud, trying to reassure herself. "It will all be fine. The Baron and the Contessa will chitchat through one more meal, then go off into their own separate, *real* worlds. And no one but her guardian angel will ever know how fiercely she was tempted to taste the delights of a one-night stand."

With renewed strength she tossed her few belongings into the small suitcase, zipped up the clothes bag Rosie had loaned her, and touched up her makeup.

Cocktails, dinner, and a polite good-bye. She could handle that much. Yes, surely she could.

Three

When Halley wandered back to the main house for cocktails an hour later, the patio and terrace were transformed into a mystery fantasyland. Low lights outlined the area and cast flickering shadows across the bricks, while in the background, soft music drifted along with the breeze. Flower arrangements dotted with tiny magnifying glasses and Sherlock Holmes hats were set on low tables, and in the center of the patio a long, lovely buffet table was draped in linen, readied for a feast.

Halley looked around. A dozen or so people milled around, chatting and drinking cocktails, but her Baron was not among them. Strange, she thought, how she knew he wasn't there even before she checked. It was all becoming too predictable, too instinctive. Too wonderful.

"Contessa, won't you join us?" An attractive blond woman wearing a sexy black dress beckoned to her. She was playing the part of a niece of the wealthy, deceased man, and her dress, Halley presumed, was her "mourning" attire.

Halley joined the group, accepted a cocktail from a maid, and was soon deep into a speculative discussion on the identity of the villain. Slips of paper and pencils were passed around on silver trays, and each guest was instructed to write down his or her conjecture about who did it and why.

"You haven't many clues, Contessa," the niece said. "What have you been doing all afternoon?"

"Keeping her Baron out of mischief," a familiar voice intoned near her ear.

Halley felt shivers travel down her neck.

The group laughed, and Don Siciliano jovially slapped Nick on the back. "Ah, to be young again!"

"Don Siciliano, you are certainly not old," Halley offered, at a loss as to what else to say.

"Thank you, my dear, thank you. But you'll notice *I* wasn't paired with a ravishing contessa!" His lined eyes sparkled with enjoyment. "It was a concentrated attempt to avoid cardiac arrest this weekend."

"Ah, Don Siciliano, they say sex is good for the heart muscle," the blonde in the black dress said teasingly.

Halley felt the flush travel up between her breasts. She knew it coated her neck and wondered if she'd soon break out all over in a sweat. "Isn't the table lovely?" she said quickly.

"It is. Let's take a closer look." Nick took her arm and smoothly led her away from the group. "Contessa, I do believe you're blushing."

"Nonsense."

"Would you like another cocktail?"

"No thank you. I have to drive home."

"I'd be happy to dr—"

"No!" Halley looked up, startled. It was the real world he was talking about now. It was intruding, and she felt suddenly sad. "I mean, I have my car here, you see. But thank you for offering."

"You know we'll be ending the masquerade shortly, Contessa. That bothers you, doesn't it?"

Halley looked up into his eyes and smiled sadly.

"Honestly? Yes, I guess it does. It has been a lovely weekend. Reality will change that."

"Why?"

"Well, because it will, that's all."

"I want to see you again, Contessa."

"See me . . . ?"

"Yes. You yourself admitted it was a wonderful weekend."

"*Lovely.* I said it was a lovely weekend."

Nick smiled and spread his fingers through the thick, lustrous hair at her neck. "All right. *Lovely* weekend."

"But it was the Baron and the Contessa who were having a lovely weekend."

"And you don't think the real people behind the Baron and the Contessa would like each other?"

"Maybe," Halley said with a soft smile. "But their worlds wouldn't be a fantasyland like this. They might find that in the light of—"

"Good evening, lovely guests!" Herb's melodious baritone hushed the crowd, and Halley's words were left dangling. She felt relieved. What else was there to say?

"While we are enjoying our cocktails and hors d'oeuvres, our detective would like to have a word with us. Monsieur?" Herb stepped back and let the short, mustached actor take center stage.

"Ladies and gentlemen, the time has come for us to weed out the chaff from the wheat." He nodded to a large man playing his assistant. "Please collect the ballots, Charles."

The crowd murmured in anticipation as pieces of paper were dropped into a silver bowl.

"We have amongst us a murderer," the actor said in heavily accented English. His small, round eyes searched the group.

Nick's fingers rubbed lightly along the side of Halley's neck, and she sighed softly.

"I see some of you are not disturbed by this." The detective raised his bushy eyebrows and looked at Halley and Nick in mock seriousness. "Perhaps that should make us suspicious. . . ."

A ripple of laughter spread through the crowd. "The Baron stood to inherit a bundle," one guest said.

"But he doesn't wear lipstick, and we found a tube of lipstick near the body," another said.

"But what about the Contessa?" Joanna, the has-been actress, countered.

"But the *motive?*" Otto Bailey asked.

"Ah, I can see you have all put deep thought into this," the detective said. "Marvelous! And we shall see shortly who is to win Mr. Harrington's grand reward of a week aboard his incredible yacht, *Seabreeze*, completely equipped with everything your heart—and that of a dozen of your closest friends—desires for pampered, sublime happiness: cook and crew, caviar, and hidden pleasures too incredible to mention!"

Again the night air filled with a rippling of pleased chatter.

"So now to business." The detective's brows drew together, and he lit a long-stemmed pipe dramatically, then continued. "We have here the deceased—Lucius A. March, wealthy entrepreneur, uncle of Janice and Melody March." He nodded to the blonde in the black dress and her "sister," a nervous woman who was trying to give up smoking and spent every waking minute knitting a long, narrow band. "And on his wife's side, uncle to the Baron von Bluster." He stretched out the last name dramatically, until all the guests were laughing. Then, one by one, the actor-detective went through the list of characters, giving each one a motive of some sort.

Halley tried hard to concentrate, but Nick's warm fingers, now gripping her waist, were building a whole other kind of anticipation within her. She felt as if fireflies danced beneath her breasts and tickling butterfly wings fluttered in her stomach. She bit down hard on her lower lip and shut her eyes tightly.

"Don't worry, my Tessa. If you did it, I'll bail you out." Nick's lips were so close to her ear, she could feel the movement of his words; it was a tantalizing sensation.

Her eyes shot open. "And you, what if *you* did it?"

"Then you bail me out. We can't lose each other again, my love." His deep, husky voice filled her fully with the fantasy. "Ah, Tessa—Monsieur Detective is about to point out the murderer." Nick dropped a kiss on the top of her head and directed her attention back to the detective.

Halley clenched her fists and fought the rushing feelings of emotion. It's not real, she shouted silently, and forced herself to concentrate on the small man entertaining the guests with a very good imitation of Hercule Poirot.

"Mr. March, our victim, had an extensive art collection, as we all know." He nodded solemnly. "You knew that, did you not, Mr. Boyles?" His gaze settled on the butler with whom Halley had had lunch and who now was standing next to her.

'Of course I did," the man answered. "I worked for the old man. I would have had to be blind not to."

The detective laughed merrily. "Blind. You weren't blind. Not only that, but you recognized great art when you saw it."

"Only because I always heard the Baron talking about how valuable it was! He coveted the collection!"

Nick's brows lifted in surprise. Halley bit back a giggle and looked up at him solemnly. "Baron, you—"

"But *I* have an alibi!" Nick smiled smugly and looked around at the guests.

Halley frowned and wondered which lovely guest would step forward.

"Our lovely hostess Sylvia Harrington and I were having a chat in the library until nearly two A.M."

The imitation Poirot nodded his head. "Absolutely true!"

Halley tilted her head to one side and looked into Nick's laughing eyes. "You could have fooled me—"

"Ah, Contessa, you don't think I'd cheat on you our first weekend together?" He kissed her soundly then, and the guests voiced delighted approval.

"The Baron was too enchanted with finding his beloved Contessa again even to have played with the idea of murder," the detective announced decisively.

"But you, Ms. March—" He pointed to Janice, the blond-haired niece dressed in black. "Where were *you* at midnight last night?"

"Me? Don't be ridiculous!" The woman's brows lifted arrogantly. She spun around and stared at her sister. "What about *her*? Melody's the one with the knitting needles!"

Melody dropped her band of yarn to the floor, her eyes wide. "Why, of all the—"

"Yes, and her knitting needles have been found all over the estate. Anyone could have picked them up. Anyone who wanted to murder someone." The detective looked again at the butler. "Anyone who might have been stealing the artwork and replacing them with forgeries, until Mr. March began to suspect—"

"It was *Janice's* idea!" the butler yelled, his arm flying out and pressing Halley back into Nick's arms.

"Welcome," Nick murmured seductively, and Halley responded with a dreamy smile.

"Of course it was," the detective continued. "Her uncle suspected her part in the forgeries and was about to cut her out of his will. By murdering him *and* implicating Melody, she'd have twice as much fortune to share with her lover, the butler! And that, my friends"—his round face broke into smiles—"is that!"

The guests' loud and appreciative applause filled the night air, and Halley felt Nick's arms encircle her, then continue to clap. She was cozily trapped, wonderfully enclosed. The smell of his after-shave blended with the night breeze, and Halley breathed it all in, savoring it, tucking it away.

Herb Harrington stepped back into the circle of guests and quieted them one final time. "And the winner of the cruise is none other than my close friend, Otto Bailey, known in real life, as most of you know, as Stan Melrose. A hand for our chief detective, please!"

Halley watched and smiled as the elderly man and his gray-haired wife walked up and hugged Herb.

"Well, good for Stan and Abbie," Nick said, half to himself. "I'll have to see that they make use of it."

Halley looked up questioningly, but Nick just smiled down at her and rubbed his chin into her hair.

"And now, folks, a final feast awaits you. Please help yourselves to the buffet and spend the remainder of the evening peeling off your disguises and getting reacquainted, now that we're back in the real world!"

Halley stiffened, and Nick pulled her away from the mingling, noisy crowd of people who were greeting each other by their familiar names.

"What's the matter?"

"Nothing." Halley tried to smile brightly. At least nothing *should* be the matter. She was blowing this out of proportion.

"Well, then, it's time to confess."

Halley took a quick lungful of air. "All right. I am Halley Finnegan."

Nick's eyes smiled. "Halley—" He said her name slowly, letting the sounds slip off his tongue only when they were ready.

Halley laughed. "Halley. Plain, simple Halley Finnegan. And you are Nick. Nick Harrington?"

He nodded. "That's right. Not the original, however. I'm the third."

"Nick Harrington the third." Halley's heart thudded. She smiled into the space between them. "I'm impressed."

"Well, I'm starved, Halley Finnegan. Shall we?" He ushered her to the enormous buffet table, which was filled with platters of smoked turkey, ham, rare roast beef, and croissants. Mustard sauces and vegetable salads wrapped in pockets of freshly baked dough rounded out the meal. The assortment was endless, and Halley filled her plate enthusiastically, finding food a much more manageable topic of concentration than Nick Harrington the third.

"Contessa—"

"Halley," she said, correcting him, as they walked over to a circle of wrought-iron chairs.

"Halley, then." Nick set his plate on the low, round table and rescued two glasses of wine from a passing waiter's tray. "Halley, I want to see you again. Tomorrow if possible."

She looked up, her forkful of turkey fluttering loosely in the air. She gulped. "Why?"

He drew his brows together dramatically. "Because, my Contessa, we have so many years to make up for—"

"Halley, remember? And, Nick, I don't think—"

Before she could finish, they were joined by several other guests, who sat down and filled the charged air with lively conversation. Halley felt a wave of relief, as if she'd been rescued from some danger. She watched as they talked, half listening to them, but mostly thinking about the irony of it all. In their disguises they had been totally free to flirt and laugh and let emotions soar. Now, within the space of a few moments, it was all different. She looked at

Nick's handsome face, then at the others in the group. Obviously they all knew each other, had grown up together, felt at ease with each other. Just as she and Rosie did, and Archie and Bridget and the people who made up *her* world. *That* was her life. This was Nick's.

Only Nick noticed when she got up from her chair. "Halley?"

She smiled down at him. "I want to see Sylvia."

"But only for a minute," he said. "Hurry back." Then he was distracted by a question from one of the others, and Halley walked off quickly. The cooling night air was refreshing, and she felt the cobwebs in her mind gently blow away. Nick was still caught in the fantasy, but logical Halley wasn't. Too bad. It was a lovely fantasy. The masquerade had been fun, but she was exhausted, and her feelings for this lovely fairy tale were growing too real to play with anymore.

No, she knew what she had to do. She'd take her money and run, as they say. Take her dreams and tuck them away, before the masquerade was dropped completely.

It would be lovely if fantasies came true, she thought as she searched for Sylvia and Herb Harrington, but they couldn't. Halley Finnegan couldn't be a contessa. No, even if fantasies could come true, she couldn't be a contessa, not by the farthest stretch of the imagination. That was the clincher, because it didn't take any imagination at all to turn Nick into a real-life baron. The thought made her strangely sad.

"It was wonderful!" she told Sylvia after Herb had sent a servant for her bags. The two stood alone on the wide fan of steps in front of the house.

"You're sure you can't stay a few more hours?" Sylvia looked genuinely disappointed.

"Yes, and I'm terribly sorry." She watched Rosie's

bags being loaded into the tiny Volkswagen that the servant had driven to the entrance. Had it been only yesterday when she'd arrived? It seemed a lifetime ago. Impulsively, she hugged Sylvia before starting down the steps.

Halfway down, she stopped and turned around.

"Yes, dear?" Sylvia said.

"I truly *did* have a wonderful time. I wonder if you'd mind telling the Baron how much I enjoyed his company, and that perhaps we'll meet again . . . maybe in Antibes?" She smiled up at her hostess.

Sylvia nodded. "Or perhaps even in Philadelphia," she said wisely.

As Halley watched, a hint of a smile lighted the older woman's face, then she turned and walked slowly back into her lovely home.

Four

Halley sat behind the desk in the tiny library office, her legs twisted around the straight wooden legs of the chair. A small smile played at the edges of her lips. She turned a page of the heavy book, and a fine puff of dust filled the air. "Ah-choo!"

"God bless you, Halley Finnegan! And where in heaven's name have you been?"

"I've been to London to visit the queen." Halley smiled up at her friend Rosie and slipped her glasses to the top of her head.

"You're not very funny, Finnegan. At the very least I deserve a full report. Those were *my* clothes, you know."

"Rosie, of that I was very, very aware. There was no way on earth they could have been mine!"

"You didn't call last night."

"I was bushed."

"How bushed? And *why* were you bushed, living in the lap of luxury for two days?" Rosie leaned against the desk and sipped coffee from a Styrofoam cup.

"You're not supposed to have coffee in the library."

"You're not supposed to have that positively X-rated,

sensuous smile on your face while you read"—she flipped over the book resting open in front of Halley—"*Post Civil War Cemeteries!* That *definitely* doesn't deserve a smile!"

"I like cemeteries. And I liked the weekend," she added softly.

"Hah! Now we're getting down to the nitty-gritty!"

"It was fantasy all the way, Rosie, but not so bad."

"Yes, yes—"

Halley stared off into space for a minute, and her friend smiled. Then, with sudden zeal, she stood and scooped up her books. "Sorry, Rosie, I'd love to chew over all the juicy details with you, but I have a meeting with the Thorne Center board this afternoon."

"Finnegan, sometimes I wonder why I put up with you."

Halley loosened one arm from under the pile of books and hugged Rosie tightly. "Me, too, but I'm awfully glad you do, because for all your ill-conceived ideas, you're quite a lovely person and a ten-plus in the friend category."

"Well," Rosie muttered, walking alongside Halley as they made their way through the main library hall and toward the front door, "you sure as hell don't treat me like a ten."

"Why don't we have dinner tonight so we can debate that?"

"I'm meeting Fred at the Grill."

"Great. I'll join you and fill you *both* in on the wild escapades of Contessa Halley Finnegan. Ciao."

"Fred agrees with me, you know," Rosie shouted after her as Halley scampered down the wide marble steps in front of the mansion that was now a library. "You need some sex in your life, Halley Finnegan. Pure, enjoyable, simple sex!"

Several sedate, elderly couples strolling the spacious estate lawns stopped to stare at the young woman who stood alone on the library steps.

Rosie smiled sweetly in their direction, lifted one shoulder in a playful shrug, then bounced down the steps and off into the sun-drenched Monday afternoon.

"So, ladies and gentlemen," Halley said, pushing her glasses back up her nose, "as you can see, the Thorne Center is quickly becoming far more than a library. The entire estate is being put to use for a variety of purposes. We now have fourteen programs in place and nearly a dozen more on the drawing board." She smiled happily, slipped off her glasses, and sat back down in the leather chair.

"I have something to add to all those numbers Ms. Finnegan's been shoving at us." The balding, elderly Leo Thorne stood up and smiled kindly at Halley. "If my father had any idea what good things that Irish lass was going to do for the neighborhood, he'd probably have given up his home years ago and moved into a bus station! A fine tribute it's become, and it's a damn shame he died before Ms. Finnegan talked me into this harebrained idea!"

Halley smiled at the white-haired man who was responsible not only for her going on to college but for her job as well. She cared deeply for Leo Thorne. He'd never been anything but wonderful to her—with the exception of coercing her into attending the Harringtons' party. *That* idea of his had cost her a sound sleep last night when she finally returned home from the Harringtons', her head filled with thoughts of barons and her heart slightly askew. She'd have to speak to her dear friend privately and let him know he owed her one.

A shuffling noise at the boardroom door caused the room to hum with muffled voices for a moment as a younger man came in and took a seat near the door. Halley squinted but couldn't make out the newcomer without her glasses. Probably another reporter, she thought. Whenever they needed a heart-warming human-interest story, they'd come to Halley, then write gushingly about "the blue-collar neighborhood surrounding the Thorne Estate which now, thanks to a few dedicated souls, has its very own library."

Another report was passed around, and Halley retrieved her glasses. One of these days, she thought as she put them on, she'd dress appropriately for these meetings. Heels, nylons, the works. Leo usually held them at his bank, and the women on the board came looking elegant. She glanced down at her long jeans skirt and big, soft overblouse. She'd slipped a belt around her waist as an afterthought that morning and suspected she looked a little like Annie Hall. She bit back a laugh. No, she wasn't the elegant type, no matter *what* fantasy she'd played out this weekend. She was plain Halley Finnegan, librarian. That's who she'd always be. But no matter, the weekend *had* been lovely. Nick the Baron had been a handsome prince who wouldn't be soon forgotten. She thought about what he'd said, about wanting to see her again, and shook her head gently. No, Baron, that is not to be . . . The thought caused a pain of regret deeper than Halley cared to admit, and she forced herself to concentrate on Leo's discourse.

"So, my fine friends, until next month, let's call it a day and get on with the business of life."

Halley lifted her head and smiled at Leo's solemn words, the same words he used to end every meeting she had ever attended. She scooped up her papers and notes, dumped them into her huge purse, and walked across the room to where Leo stood chatting with a small group.

He winked at her over the head of several people,

but it was when the group parted that she realized the reason for the wink.

Standing next to Leo, looking every bit as elegant as he had in her dreams, stood her Baron.

Her heart thudded uncontrollably. "You!"

Nick grinned. "Me."

"Here?"

"Yes."

"Why?"

Nick smiled.

"Well, now, this is one of the most fascinating conversations I've been privy to for some time!" Leo clapped Nick on the back familiarly.

"Leo . . . why is he here?" Halley pushed her glasses up until they nested comfortably in her hair. Little did Leo know that monosyllables and simple sentences were absolutely all she was capable of right now.

"Personal invitation, my dear."

"So you know Nick, then." It wasn't a question, but somehow Halley felt a need to state the obvious. Then she'd know whether this was a part of the dreams that moved her in and out of sleep all night, or real, true life.

Nick stood quietly, his eyes carefully recording every inch of her, and suddenly Halley realized why. Although *he* still looked every inch the Baron— immaculately groomed, wearing an expensive three-piece suit, his thick hair carefully combed—*she* was Cinderella at her hearth.

"Leo is a good friend of my uncle's."

"Of course," she murmured, remembering why she had been at the party in the first place. She pushed a wayward strand of hair back in place while she collected her thoughts.

"I told you I wanted to see you again, and you were about as difficult to find as the Statue of Liberty."

"Find? I wasn't lost, Nick."

"You ran off."

"Oh, no, really, I—"

"And you didn't leave a slipper. But I had this and wondered if it fit." He pulled the flowing emerald-green scarf from his pocket.

Halley looked at it and thought of sweet-smelling woods and a lovely, passionate kiss. Her laughter was soft as she fingered the silky material. "No, actually it *doesn't* fit. It belonged to a contessa. But as you can plainly see, she's not here."

Her smile was warm and honest, and Nick wondered briefly what the hell was happening to him. He hadn't slept much the night before. In half sleep, his arms had reached out for a beautiful, enchanting contessa, and his lips had yearned for the sweetness she held. She had haunted his thoughts for hours, like a beautiful, magical witch.

Now he was here, standing in front of her again. From a distance she had seemed plain compared to the ravishing, sexy beauty of the previous day's contessa. He'd almost walked out for a moment, certain that he had made a mistake. But up close she was every bit as beautiful—even with those crazy horn-rimmed glasses that stuck out from her wind-blown hair like a visor. It was a different kind of beauty, and the sensuality was softer but definitely still there. Her freckles were more prominent without makeup, but the lovely curves he had traced with his hands were still the same, even with the layers of clothing she wore and the denim skirt that dipped way below her knees. Like a fine fabric, the blended, woven lines of her were even more lovely up close.

"Oh, but the Contessa *is* here." Nick fingered a lock of hair that fell over her shoulder.

Leo Thorne coughed loudly. "Excuse me, you two, but I have business to attend to." He edged his way to the door.

"Leo, wait! Isn't Nick here to see you?"

"No, my lovely. He and I talked before the board meeting. Oh, and Halley?"

"Yes?"

"I promised Nick you'd take him on a tour of the Thorne Estate. He was fascinated by what we've done out there."

"But, Leo—"

"I'd do it myself, but I have another meeting, and you do such a good job of showing the old place off, you know."

Leo's swift movement through the door belied his seventy years. Halley watched him silently, her hasty objection left hanging like the last leaf of autumn on a barren branch.

"Do you mind?" Nick's rich voice filled the empty room.

"Well . . ."

"We're not strangers, you know."

"But in a way we are, Nick. The weekend was just a game, pretending. I'm someone different. I'm Halley—"

"Yes, you are. Halley Elizabeth Mary Finnegan."

She glanced up at him, a slow smile spreading across her face. "But what's in a name? Do you know, also, that I'm not really a contessa?"

"I don't know that at all." Nick wrapped an arm around her and steered her out the front door of the bank. "You're my denim-clad contessa. I think it's rather nice."

"But not chic, Nick. Not chic at all. Or glamorous." She put her glasses back on and looked up into the deep black eyes. Oh, my, he was handsome! she thought. "I'm a—"

"Librarian. Leo told me." His fingers played with the hair at her neck, and he found himself wanting to play with far more. "I've never met a librarian before. I mean, person-to-person—"

Halley laughed and shook her hair free. "We're a fascinating breed."

Her freckles deepened when she laughed, and Nick was enchanted. "I know."

"To add a serious touch to this conversation, Mr. Harrington, what the devil are you doing here?"

Nick held open the door of a Porsche 944, and Halley slipped inside, inhaling the wonderful leathery smell. She could smell Nick, too—his sexy, musky after-shave smelled like those envelope samples from Giorgio's that passed across her desk at the library.

Nick was around the car and beside her in seconds. "I told you. I came to see you."

Halley looked straight ahead, trying to keep her smile appropriate. To see *her*? Crazy! A man with a III behind his name didn't pursue someone like Halley Finnegan! She shifted in the seat to look at him, and when she read the seriousness in his eyes, her laughter spilled out. "Oh, Nick . . ."

Nick's smile was confused. "I didn't know I was so funny." He started the engine and steered the car into the line of traffic.

"I'm sorry, Nick. It's simply a surprise. I didn't really expect to see you again."

"Are you disappointed?"

She shook her head and pointed directions toward the tiny pocket of the town that housed the neighborhood known as the Hill. "Of course not."

"Good—although I would have come, anyway." His hand moved over and rested on her thigh.

Halley continued to give directions, ignoring the searing heat that lit her up like a Christmas tree. She prayed he wouldn't notice. Lord, he'd think she was some sex-starved juvenile and not a twenty-seven-year-old woman who simply reacted very strongly to his touch. Like food or smells or music—some turned you on, some didn't. It certainly wasn't personal.

"The Thorne Estate is on Jackson Avenue at the top of the Hill."

"I know. We went there once when we were kids and the Thornes still lived there. A Christmas party, I think, with the biggest Christmas tree I'd ever seen in my life."

"I remember when the Thornes used to do that," Halley said softly. "All the kids in the neighborhood would try to climb the fences and hide behind bushes to see the fine cars coming up the drive." She laughed. "I got caught once by the gardener and thought I'd die. Somehow my torrent of tears softened his heart and he let me go."

"I can imagine!" Nick laughed. "So you grew up around here?"

Halley nodded. "Born and bred on the Hill." She looked out the window at the neatly kept white frame houses and small, familiar stores. It was a world in itself, old, comfortable, secure, and light-years away from the world of Nicholas Harrington.

"Well, looks like we're here." Nick slowed the car and turned onto a tree-lined, curving drive that led up to the great mansion. He followed it slowly, taking in the small roads that led off to the gate house, the greenhouse, and the stables. "I remember now," he said as memories flooded back.

They'd all come to the Thorne Christmas party. All the wealthy leaders of the city, as well as their wives and children, had come to the lower-class neighborhood where Leo Thorne had staunchly remained in the huge estate left him by his father. They'd driven through the neighborhood on their way to the party, and Nick remembered watching the kids playing on street corners and having snowball fights. And he remembered, all these years later, being struck by the porches. Every house had a friendly porch that stretched wide across the front of it, and in the dead of winter, rocking chairs and gliders still sat there empty, except for a coating of snow that made them look like pieces of sculpture. He shook his head. Funny the memories he'd hung on to . . .

"The library is on the main floor of the house," Halley said, forcing his memory to fade. He parked the car at the turn in the wide drive and they got out.

"It's amazing how everything has been kept intact."

"That was one of Leo's goals when we started planning all this. When his father died, neither Leo nor his brothers and sisters wanted the house, but no one wanted to sell it, because they were afraid it would be torn down and the land divided up. That's when we thought of the library. Keeping everything intact was a priority for all of us who were involved. Come, let me show you."

She took his arm, and together they walked up the wide marble steps. The leaded glass doors were held open today to catch the pleasant fall breezes, and the two walked into what was once the entry hall of the Thorne's family home. It was huge and elegant and now housed the main library desk that Leo had carefully selected. The dark, highly polished wood perfectly matched the woodwork and looked like a part of the house. Behind the desk was the door to Halley's office, and to the right and left were warm, spacious parlors that now housed thousands of volumes of books. She led Nick through every room, explaining as she went. They toured the small rooms in the back, which were used for reading, and on the upper floors they moved in and out of bedroom suites that now hosted meetings and craft groups, art classes and reading clubs.

"Well, do you recognize it all?" Halley asked as they returned to the main entry hall.

Her expression lovingly reflected the pride she had in the library, and Nick smiled. "Strangely enough, I do. You've done a beautiful job." He walked over to the winding staircase and looked up at the glistening chandelier. When he turned back to Halley, she was standing by the huge desk, shuffling through a pile of messages the assistant librarian had handed her.

"Looks like you work hard, Ms. Librarian."

Halley looked at him over the rim of her glasses and nodded. "It's a Finnegan trait. A curse, my mother says. We're not content unless we're knee-deep in some project or another."

"So this is your project . . ."

Halley didn't answer. Her attention had shifted to a muddy-shoed, freckle-faced six-year-old who had rushed in the door and stuck his small, square body between the two of them.

"Aunt Halley?"

"Yes, Mickey?"

"It's Archie."

Halley sighed. "Oh, no."

"Yep."

"Where is he?" Halley asked.

"Back near Whisper Cloud's grave."

Halley was already halfway to the door. "Mickey, have Kate heat up some strong coffee and bring it out back, will you, please?"

Mickey dashed off without another word. Nick was left standing alone for a brief moment, then he turned and hurried after Halley.

"Whisper Cloud's grave? Archie? I have a feeling I didn't get the whole tour, Halley."

"Well, you will now," Halley tossed back over one shoulder as she hurried around the corner of the huge house and headed out toward a large wooded area in the distance.

Just beyond the first clump of trees was a low fence, and beyond that was a scattering of neat, well kept graves.

"A cemetery?"

"Post Civil War," Halley called out proudly as she weaved her way expertly around grave markers. "It's a lovely cemetery, Nick. The Thornes' ancestors are buried here, along with other families. I grew up playing hide-and-seek here and visiting the ghosts of Indians and soldiers." She ducked beneath the low branch of an old oak. "Whisper Cloud is buried over there, beyond those maple trees." She pointed, then hurried along through streams of sunlight.

A low, gravelly moan met them as they wound their way between the trees. "I assumed Whisper Cloud—whoever the hell *he* is—was dead." Nick muttered to the widening space between himself and Halley. Then, as the peculiar feeling of adventure sparked his soul, he gave pursuit and caught up with her just as the trees thinned out.

She was standing beside a small grave, her glasses pushed to the top of her head again, her small fists dug into her narrow waist.

Settled in a huge lump between the square marker and a giant maple tree was the bulbous form of a man. Nick drew closer and stared down at the still figure.

"Oh, Archie," Halley murmured softly.

One wrinkled eyelid opened with difficulty, and through a bloodshot eye, the man peered blearily up in Nick's direction. "Good evening, sir. Have we met?"

Nick smiled as Halley crouched down, and shook her head.

"It's not evening, Archie, it's late afternoon. The gentleman is Nick Harrington, and you are dangerously close to lying atop Whisper Cloud's grave, as well as frightening the children half to death. What am I to do with you?"

A whimsical smile played across the man's puffy face. "Lemme shleep, Finnegan." His heavy lids closed.

"Archie, here." Mickey appeared from behind Nick's long legs with a cup of steaming black coffee held tightly in his small hands. He grinned up at Halley. "Kate says it's three days old and sure to wake him and put hair on his chest too!" He handed Halley the coffee and grinned up at Nick. "Sometimes Archie feels under the weather, you know."

Nick nodded as if he had some understanding of what was going on here, and hunkered down next to Halley. "Here, I'll do that." He slipped his arm behind Archie's wide shoulders and forced him forward while Halley lifted the cup to his lips and began forcing the black, syrupy liquid down his throat.

"Nish." Archie winked at Halley.

"Very," Halley said. "But you're not. Drink this, my friend. You know such celebrating is taboo on library grounds."

"Shorry, Finnegan." His head rolled forward, and Nick had to bite back a grin at the man's solemn contriteness.

"I mean it, Archie." Halley sat back on her legs and tried to look stern.

The deep belching sounds Archie made in response brought a huge grin to Mickey's face, but it was wiped away by one look from Halley.

"Mickey, maybe you can talk Kate into fixing Archie some soup. Nick can help me get him over to the stable."

"Okay. See ya in a minute, Arch."

Mickey flew off again, and Halley rose. "Archie has a room in the stable. Do you mind, Nick?"

"Certainly not."

In seconds he had Archie to his feet and had hoisted a limp arm around his own shoulder, the other around Halley's. "Most interesting Monday I've spent in some time," he said as they made their way along the path.

"This isn't how barons usually start their week?" Halley nudged Archie to take another step.

"Ah, it's confession time, Contessa . . ."

"You're really a library inspector of some sort, and we're about to lose our status."

Nick grinned. "That's not exactly what I've come to inspect."

"I, sir, am a gentleman bum," Archie interjected with a crooked grin, his words slurring together. "Try it, you'll like it."

"From baron to bum. Hmm, it has possibilities, especially if it means having the Contessa so close."

"Contesh . . . ?" Archie tried to hold his head straight.

"Ms. Finnegan."

"Finnegan. Ah, she's a queen, a woman of beauty, a—"

"Hush, Archie. You're drunk."

"Merely tipsy, my lovely. . . ."

"He makes sense to me." Nick pushed open the stable door with his hip and helped Archie through. "Where to?"

"The back room. There's a cot there," Halley directed, and in minutes Nick had the hobo situated in the small room that was filled with colorful children's drawings, a small table and chair, and a cot.

"Home shweet home." Archie sank back on the cot, and his eyelids lowered immediately.

Halley took Nick's arm and drew him out of the room and back outdoors. "Thanks."

"My pleasure." He looked down at Halley. *She* was his pleasure, a *great* pleasure, and he set his jaw, fighting the urge to wrap her in his arms. "Who *is* he?"

"He's Archie, that's all. Friend, hobo, teacher of life." She smiled softly. "He likes it here, and we've become attached to him. So he stays. He spends a lot of time in the gazebo holding court with the kids. But every now and then—"

"I see." Nick shoved his hands deep into the pockets of his tailored pants and fell in step beside her as they walked slowly back to the library. "And the little boy?"

"My sister Bridget's son. He and Archie are good buddies."

"And last but not least . . ."

"Whisper Cloud is an Indian girl buried in the cemetery. Archie weaves tales about her and her tribe for the kids." She laughed and tilted her head back to let the late-afternoon sun warm her face. "All of us have gotten attached to Whisper Cloud. . . ."

Nick didn't hear the last sentence. When she tilted her head back like that and he fell into the clear, green sea of her eyes, all resolve melted. He touched the back of her neck and lifted his fingers into her hair. "Oh, Tessa—"

"*Halley*, Nick. You're confusing—"

But all confusion was blotted out when his lips covered hers, softly at first, then with a crush of familiarity. He'd know his Contessa blindfolded, Nick thought vaguely. No one else in the universe could taste this sweet, feel this soft and tender beneath his touch. His kiss turned greedy, and his tongue slipped between her lips. *His* Contessa . . . yes, it made an irrational kind of sense. . . .

It was Halley who finally pulled away. "You don't step out of character easily, do you, Nicholas the third?"

"And you fall into it quite readily, Contessa."

Halley nodded, and a small smile touched her lips. "I guess I do. But I know deep down that Irish librarians make terrible contessas in real life. Do you know that?"

Nick couldn't imagine her ever backing away from the truth. Not with those eyes. He nodded slowly. "Contessas are a dime a dozen, but Irish librarians—now there's a find."

"Who are *you*, anyway?" Halley asked. Nick's arm had gone around her, and they started to walk again, their hips gently touching as they moved along the leaf-covered path.

"Nicholas Harrington, Philadelphia—"

"Main Line."

"Sh. You asked the question, I answer. I own banks and live alone. I like to travel, don't cook, and drive too fast. I'm moody and a little spoiled by people who worry too much about me, but beneath it all I'm not too bad a guy."

Halley poked him in the ribs, and her burst of laughter caught on the breeze. Nick drew her closer. Halley Finnegan. Librarian. Crazy . . .

"I guess that's it, then." Halley moved out of his embrace as they neared the sprawling house.

"That's it?"

"The Cook's tour. Except for the cottage where I live, and the garages, you've seen it all."

"Are you free for dinner?"

Halley paused for a moment, then regretfully shook her head. She'd promised Rosie, and besides, Nick might still be living in the fantasy of the weekend. Now that he'd seen her as she really was, a plain, blue-collar neighborhood librarian, he might need to think about that. . . . "I . . . I'm sorry, Nick. I already have plans."

"Is there a man in your life?" he asked bluntly.

"No, no, it's not that. I promised a good friend—"

Nick watched her closely as she took one step up toward the library entrance. She paused, then turned back to him, the soft denim of her skirt flapping soundlessly against her ankles. She pulled her glasses off her head and slipped them on her nose. "There. Now you're in focus again. It *was* good to see you again, Nick. Thank you for coming, and for the invitation. Good-bye."

Nick shook his head, and the smile that softened his face was more natural than anything he'd felt in a long, long time. "No, Contessa Finnegan. Not good-bye . . ."

She smiled at him and turned away. His words warmed her back as she continued up the wide steps, and then the warmth spread to other places.

All right, fine. Her practical mind took over as she reached the cool entry hall. It would be nice to have the Baron come back. But she knew, even if he didn't, that he'd linger in her world of dusty books and the Dewey decimal system about as long as she would in the jet-setting world of murder-mystery weekends.

"Halley, what I wouldn't give to read minds right now!" Elderly Kate Willows, her assistant, stood behind the desk with a wide smile on her face.

Halley tossed her hair and laughed. "I was simply speculating on the overused aphorism that some spots are very nice to visit, but, as they say . . ."

"Hmm." Kate frowned skeptically. "If you say so. But judging by that dreamy expression I'd swear vacations weren't on your mind."

Halley only sighed.

Outside, Nick watched her for a moment, then walked slowly back to his car. A librarian, of all the incredible things. He shook his head and saw Mickey dashing away from the house, a wrapped basket held tightly in his hands. Archie's sobering-up food, Nick guessed.

Suddenly Nick stiffened.

The cemetery.

He had stood in a cemetery, and the air had not been squeezed from his lungs; icy fingers hadn't prodded him, stung him, numbed him. He rubbed the car keys between his fingers and drew his eyebrows together.

Fading sunlight through the distant tree branches directed his thoughts from one unseen grave to the next: to Whisper Cloud's . . . to the Thorne ancestors . . . to other graves in other cemeteries . . . and inevitably to Anne's. But he had done it; he had stood beside Halley in a cemetery, and memory had not cut into his life.

As he shielded his eyes and looked off into the distance, Nick felt a lifting sensation, a sweet wash of comfort. It didn't make sense, but it was there.

In the four years since he'd buried Anne Melrose Harrington, Nick hadn't been able to pass a cemetery without feeling her loss with a pain that reached to the deepest part of him and left him lifeless. He had vowed on the day of his wife's burial never to set foot in a cemetery again. They housed too much anguish, too many memories. Nick felt the sting of pain now as he stood alone, staring off toward the sunset. But the sting was manageable, and the burning glow of the setting sun was still there when he looked again.

And it was lovely.

Five

Halley walked slowly through the tiny living room of her cottage, enjoying the play of sunlight on the braided rug her grandmother had given her. The rich reds, oranges, and blues of thick wool scraps were a vibrant match for the trees outside her window. Even the dancing dust motes looked good in the golden light, Halley decided, so she'd be generous and not disturb them today.

"Halley, are you in there?"

"Patience, my dear Rosie, patience."

Rosie tumbled through the door when Halley finally unlocked it. Her cheeks were as pink as the warm-up clothes she wore. "It took you ages to get to the door, Finnegan. Was I . . . ah, interrupting anything?"

Halley laughed halfheartedly at the expectant sparkle in Rosie's eyes. "Sorry to disappoint you, Rosie. I was making my bed, not hiding a man under it."

Rosie frowned. "A friend can hope, can't she?"

"I suppose. You're up early for a Saturday. Sit down."

Rosie sprawled on the couch and folded her legs beneath her. She pulled a newspaper out from un-

der her arm and handed it to Halley. "I have a confession to make."

Halley took the newspaper and began scanning
the front page while she waited for Rosie to go on.

"I was beginning to doubt the reality of this baron,
Halley."

"Rosie, if I'm sure of anything in life, it's that Nick
Harrington is real."

"However, he hasn't come back," Rosie tossed out.
"But now I know why."

Halley looked up from the paper. "Oh?" It was true
he hadn't come back all week, and although she was
surprised at the intensity of her disappointment,
Halley was determined to put it aside. After all, why
should he come back? A man like Nick Harrington
certainly had many more things to do than hang
around libraries.

"Yes, I do." Rosie's pretty face was lit by a
smile. "At least if your Baron is the *same* Nicholas
Harrington—"

"Same as what, Rosie?" Halley had inched to the
end of the chair and dropped the newspaper to the
floor.

"Same as the one on page three of the newspaper."

Halley stared at the paper.

"Well?"

Slowly she picked it up and turned to page three.
His picture was near the top, his name a part of the
headline, but the rest of the words were a blur. It
was only his face that stayed in focus. It was as
handsome as the image she carried around with
her, but for the first time she noticed the edge to his
smile, the detached look in those lovely black eyes.
Had he looked like that when they kissed? she wondered. No, she was sure he hadn't.

"He just closed a deal on a bank in Chicago,"
Rosie announced with authority.

"Oh." Halley looked at the tall, lean body in the

picture. He had on a tuxedo, just like her Baron. Her breath caught in her throat, and she felt the stirrings inside again.

"Halley, you're blushing!"

"It's hot in here." She dropped the newspaper to the floor and smiled weakly. "So now you know he's real. And you also know why he hasn't been around. And you *also* know why he'll probably never show up again."

The strong knock on the door was unexpected. Once Halley unlocked her door in the morning, people usually dispensed with formalities and simply walked in and made themselves at home. "You're expecting someone?"

Halley shook her head.

The second knock was even stronger and roused Halley from the couch.

Outside, Nick stood patiently on the step, his hands shoved in his pants pockets and his thoughts centered on the woman he hoped would be on the other side of the door. She'd been on his mind all week. There was something about Halley that had distracted him in meetings at the bank, had followed him to Chicago, and crept up on him when he wasn't expecting it. He needed to see her again, to find out what this was all about, to work it out of his system.

When Halley finally opened the door, Nick's hand was raised, ready to knock again.

"Don't knock on air, it's bad luck," Halley said softly.

"An old Irish saying, no doubt."

She nodded. "Come in."

"Yes, do!"

Halley looked over her shoulder at Rosie. She was still on the couch, but her neck was stretched to its maximum length.

Nick strode into the cheery room and smiled politely at Rosie. "Hello, I'm Nick Harrington."

"Yes, you certainly are. Never, ever could you be a figment of someone's imagination."

Nick's eyebrows lifted in puzzlement.

"Don't mind Rosie, Nick. She had her doubts as to your existence."

His deep laughter filled the small room. "Well, I'm sure there are ways to prove it," he said as he looked over at Halley with a sexy grin.

"It's okay. She believes in you now," she said hastily.

"Do you?"

"Absolutely." Rosie knew that much, that he was real, but she wouldn't bet her life savings on anything more about Nick Harrington. "So, what are you doing here?"

"Oh, I just happened to be in the neighborhood."

Rosie hooted. "Come now, Nick, anyone as exotically handsome as you ought to be able to come up with something more imaginative than that! Sit down here and tell me about yourself, starting with the day you were born, and don't leave out one juicy detail."

Rosie's smile went from ear to ear, and her eyebrows were raised in delicious anticipation.

Halley laughed. "Rosie's shy. Have a seat, Nick."

Nick stepped over the newspaper still littering the floor and sat down next to Rosie. He glanced down at the paper and spotted the page-three headline. "Hmm, looks like I've been under foot around here."

"Good!" Rosie beamed. "He has a sense of humor. That's very important."

"For what?" Nick asked.

"For courting my dear friend Halley."

"Rosemary Agnes Wilson!" Halley barked out.

Nick looked from one woman to the other, then leaned his head back into a slanted ray of sunshine and smiled. There was a tonic being dished out here in Halley's small cottage that agreed with him. "You know, I think Rosemary Agnes and I understand each other."

"For that kind remark, Nick the Baron, I will leave you two alone and run along to open the store. We'll save the life story for another day." Rosie pecked him on the cheek and gave him a quick hug.

Halley watched from across the room. Nick was still smiling, but he'd stiffened slightly when Rosie surprised him with her hug. Rosie was warm and spontaneous in showering affection on anyone she liked. Nick, Halley guessed as she watched him closely, wasn't used to people like Rosie. Well, it didn't matter. No one could be around Rosie for more than a few seconds and not like her. "Rosie manages a vintage clothing store," Halley filled in quickly as her friend walked across the room. "It's wonderful."

"Yes, it is," Rosie agreed. "And it's from that very store, Nick, that your Contessa was clothed."

"Well, then it must be terrific. My Contessa was the loveliest lady at the party. You did a superb job, Rosie."

Rosie looked over at the oversize man's shirt Halley wore and frowned. "It's too bad she won't allow me to give her advice on a daily basis."

Nick followed her glance. He hadn't even noticed what Halley was wearing and realized in that moment how little it mattered. She'd be beautiful in anything. Or nothing . . . As a matter of fact, he'd much prefer the latter.

"Rosie, go." Halley pointed toward the door.

"Beneath that dictatorial exterior lies a very sensuous woman," Rosie assured Nick as she disappeared through the door.

"That, Rosemary Agnes, is not news," Nick murmured, his eyes still lingering on Halley's shirt while his imagination slowly peeled it away.

"Nick, it's nice of you to drop by like this but—"

"I thought maybe we could spend the day together. You know, for old times' sake."

Halley busied herself picking up newspapers and empty glasses from the floor that had been left there by a group of friends who had stopped by the night before to watch an old movie on television.

"That's a very nice gesture, but I have a long list of things that have to be done today." She smiled with real regret. It would be wonderful spending a whole day with Nick, a day without masquerade. He'd probably melt into a puddle of nothingness from boredom, but it would have been nice, nevertheless. "I don't work at the library on Saturdays, you see, so I save that day for everything else."

"I'll help. Or quietly blend into the shadows. I won't be a problem."

Halley laughed. "I didn't think you'd be a problem, I simply thought you'd be bored. Come along if you like, and don't say I didn't warn you."

Halley always began her Saturdays with a huge breakfast of sausage and thick, syrupy slices of French toast at her sister Bridget's house. She considered skipping it today, but a growl from beneath the faded blue shirt convinced her otherwise. When Nick offered to wait at the library, she assured him vehemently that there was always extra food on Bridget's table and that her sister would be offended if she knew Halley had left him behind.

The white frame house was filled with kids, and Mickey quickly claimed Nick as his find while the others focused all their energies on Halley, whom they obviously adored.

"Halley is my salvation," Bridget explained as her four-year-old twins each whispered in one of Halley's ears at the same time. "She listens to them, they listen to her."

Nick nodded as he watched the redheaded youngsters giggle over something Halley had said, and a twinge of sadness swept through him.

But in Bridget Sullivan's house sadness didn't linger long. In minutes everyone was seated around a huge oak table, thanking the Lord as quickly as possible for the food, then passing it back and forth with the speed and agility of a Steelers quarterback.

Nick was friendly but quiet, Halley noticed, and no one but she seemed to sense he was uncomfortable. Well, that wasn't unusual, she decided. The Finnegan-Sullivan clan could be overwhelming at times.

The hug Bridget gave Nick as he and Halley were leaving was as natural as a handshake, and this time Nick didn't seem surprised, although he didn't return it, Halley saw.

He held the door open for her and smiled politely. "Wonderful breakfast," he said. "Thanks."

"Listen, Nick, we're happy to have you. Halley's friends are always welcome here. She knows that. Now you do too." Her round cheeks glowed.

Halley bent and kissed each of the kids, then followed Nick out of the door.

Next stop was Joe's Auto Repair.

"Are you having trouble with your car?" Nick asked, listening to the hum of the Volkswagen engine.

"Not really," Halley answered as she turned the car onto a busier street, which served as a tiny business area for the Hill district. "You happen to be riding in the most pampered bug in Philadelphia."

Nick threaded his fingers behind his head and watched her as she talked. She was perfectly relaxed, uninhibited, comfortable. Her hair moved freely about her shoulders, and she frequently brushed it back with a flick of her long, slender fingers. They were simple movements, but the tightening they caused inside of him was anything but simple. She shifted behind the wheel, and the loose shirt grew taut across her breasts for a moment, clearly outlining the full curves. He thought of them filling his palms, firming beneath his touch. He imagined the sweet excitement of kissing them.

Halley was still talking and didn't notice his quick intake of breath.

He thought of the vacation trip to Majorca that he'd suddenly canceled a couple of days ago. His hosts hadn't understood. Hell, it was no wonder; *he* hadn't understood.

"Joe likes to check it out each week," Halley continued. "Mostly it's an excuse, I think, so I'll be sure to stop by— "

Nick pushed his thoughts aside and focused on the conversation. "Joe?"

"Pop." Halley pointed to a large wooden sign fronting an auto-repair shop and slowed the car. JOE'S GARAGE, it read. "Joe is Joseph Conor Finnegan. My father," she added proudly, then honked three times. The garage door lifted and she drove on through.

Joe Finnegan was a crusty Irishman with a sparkle in his clear blue eyes. He welcomed Nick and carefully scrutinized him at the same time, but only after he had swallowed his auburn-haired daughter in a huge bear hug that lifted her clear off the cluttered cement floor.

"Pop is the best mechanic this side of the Atlantic," Halley announced, one arm looped affectionately around her dad's waist.

Joe Finnegan's rumbling laugh blotted out the compliment, and he started in on Halley's hidden virtues.

"She could replace shock absorbers before she graduated from St. Elizabeth's grade school," he said, boasting.

Nick thought of the friends he had deserted who were by now lolling on white beaches drinking expensive champagne. To them shock absorbers were small pills and analysts' couches. He forced back a smile. "I'll have to remember that."

"You take a look-see around, Nick, while Halley and I check out the vehicle. Time for the Green Knight's weekly checkup. There's coffee in my office."

His last words were muffled as he and Halley slid under the car on wheeled dollies and began poking and probing.

Nick wandered into the small office that was separated from the main garage by a dusty glass window and poured himself a cup of coffee. All he could see of Halley were her long legs sticking out from beneath the car and the flaps of her shirt resting on angled hipbones. A tiny sliver of pale skin poked through just above the jeans where the shirt pulled to the side, and Nick meditated on it for a minute. Lovely, just lovely. The next movement of her slender body caused it to disappear, and Nick satisfied himself by looking around the cluttered office.

The desktop was littered with papers and framed pictures, as were the two bookshelves along the wall. In between, covering the three walls, were more framed pictures and certificates. Nick moved closer. He picked out Halley immediately in the family group shots, even though there were several siblings that shared her coloring and one who had the same intriguing, infectious smile. There were no formal shots; even when it looked like the whole family was collected, there wasn't a stillness and stiffness about the photos. There was always someone laughing broadly, and in one or two there was a baby in tears, a solicitous adult cuddling it. He spotted Joe's garage license, framed and hanging above a picture. In the center of the whole gallery, hanging in a gilded frame and with a wide space around it so no one could miss it, was a diploma.

Nick looked closer.

Halley Elizabeth Mary Finnegan
Bachelor of Arts
Pennsylvania State University

There was a date and a scholastic honor listed on it, and Nick noticed it was the only item in the room that looked like it got a regular dusting. He smiled. The diploma was definitely important to someone.

"Hi there. We're finished." Halley breezed into the room, then stopped just inside the door. "Oh, dear, you've had to sit here alone with nothing to keep you company but Dad's Rogue's Gallery."

"I enjoyed every minute of it, Halley Summa Cum—"

"Oh, that." She blushed and wiped a grease-stained hand on a rag beside the door. "Dad insists on keeping it there. I was the first Finnegan to graduate from college, and he and his Irish pride want the world to 'damn well know it.' "

"The date should make you about twenty-four years old. . . ." Nick lifted his eyebrows mischievously.

Halley shook her head and laughed. "The Baron is diplomatic. Obviously I worked for a while first. Then, with Leo Thorne's encouragement and support, I went back on a scholarship, got in a few graduate courses so I'd know what I was doing at the Thorne Library, and went from Penn State to the Thorne Estate."

"Just like that?"

Halley clicked her fingers. "Just like that. Leo opened many doors in my life," she added softly.

Nick nodded. He was beginning to realize the importance of the diploma.

"So you see," Halley said brightly, "my life has been happy and normal . . . until one night not too long ago when I went off to a murder and landed in the arms of a baron—"

"And he swept you away into a world of sensuous pleasure."

Halley crooked one eyebrow.

"Well," Nick amended begrudgingly, "he *wanted* to sweep you off. . . . *Still* wants to."

Their laughter collided in the suddenly charged air. Nick's was firm and decisive, Halley's a blend of embarrassment and sudden shyness.

"Well, Nick." Joe appeared in the doorway and saved both of them before contemplating what to say next. "Anytime you have car trouble, bring the beast in and I'll give her a once-over."

"Thanks, Mr. Finne—"

"Joe. Everyone calls me Joe or Finn. Even the kids."

"Joe it is, then." Nick shook his hand politely, and Halley motioned toward the door. She was overdosing Nick with family; she could see it in his face. It never occurred to Halley that someone might be ill at ease around those she loved, but it *was* a different world for Nick. Was that it? Was that what was causing the lines across his handsome forehead to deepen?

She dismissed the idea almost as soon as it crossed her mind. Nick Harrington, whatever he might be, was not a snob.

"Wait, Halley." Her father stopped her at the door. "Don't rush the gentleman out so fast. Has he seen the diploma, I wonder now?"

"Pop, how could he miss it?" Halley laughed and kissed him warmly on the cheek. "He's duly impressed, I'm sure. See you tomorrow. Give Mom my love."

"You'll have to excuse Joe," Halley said as she backed the car out of the garage and into the street.

"Some things are dear to his heart. My degree happens to be one of them."

"He's nice."

"Very."

Nick was quiet as Halley drove. He didn't even ask where they were going. Joe Finnegan was on his mind, along with those pictures. All the love that leapt from one person's eyes to the next, the hugs and smiles, was so foreign to him—and the simple pride that lit Joe's tired eyes when he looked at his summa cum laude daughter. Nick suspected his pride would have been as strong if the diploma had been for finishing a speed-reading course.

The next several hours were a whirlwind. Nick declined to get out of the car at most of the places Halley stopped to do errands. These people were engulfing him too quickly. He didn't know how to respond. He didn't know *how*. . . . The thought clouded his mind as he watched Halley dash into a school supply store to pick up a bunch of games she needed for the toddlers' room at the library; as he watched her greet the postmaster with a warm hug when she picked up a stack of library mail; as he watched her sweet-talk a printer into sending over his "extra" sheets of paper for an art class at the library that she wanted to offer senior citizens. Many of the library patrons had never had such opportunities, Halley explained to her captive audience as Nick tried to find room in her tiny car for his cramped legs. Many residents of the Hill never finished high school, she went on, and now, finally, they could fill in some of their time with satisfying activities.

Then her attention switched to the orange marbled sky, and she smiled brilliantly, swallowed up by the beauty of it, until Nick had to remind her that the light had changed and there was a string of cars behind them.

In spite of his uneasiness in this world in which

she moved so naturally, Halley herself was filling him with a sweet pleasure that defied any explanation. Her pride touched him, her delight aroused him, her closeness drove him crazy, and by six-thirty that evening, Nick couldn't stand it anymore.

"Halley, stop right here. Pull over."

"Nick, what's the matter?" Her voice lifted in alarm, and she immediately pulled the car over to the edge of the deserted drive leading to the library.

"This is what's the matter."

Before she could get her foot off the brake, Nick had taken off her glasses and wound his fingers into her thick hair. In a fraction of a second his lips were devouring hers, pressing again and again with all the pent-up desire of the day. Nick tasted Halley's small gasp of surprise, and it aroused him even more. His tongue slipped effortlessly through her parted lips and began to explore the sweetness he'd remembered and dreamed about.

Halley's response came quickly and without thought, her hands circling around behind his head and digging into the thick black hair at the base of his neck. "Oh, Nick," she whispered softly.

But Nick's searching tongue prohibited discussion of the matter and slowly, lovingly, he slipped one hand beneath the lower edges of her shirt and touched the silky smooth skin beneath.

Halley moaned but didn't move away. His lips continued to move rhythmically against hers, while his fingers left heated trails across her stomach and up the delicate skin at her side. Her bra was a thin stretch of cotton and lace, and Nick quickly released the small snap hidden in the valley between her breasts. They were magnicent, round and soft and silky smooth. He cupped one, then the other, in his large hand, and Halley's head fell back as she surrendered to the delight of his touch.

Her mind stopped then, and she kissed Nick back

hungrily, loving the taste and feel and strength of him, and wishing against the wall of reason that it would never end.

A rippling movement swept through her, so real that she smiled into his kiss. "You're making me imagine I'm on a cloud, drifting along . . ."

Nick nuzzled kisses into the soft skin of her neck. "A cloud, huh? A magical . . . Oh, hell!"

Halley's eyes shot open at the nonsensical words just in time to see a clump of white pines pass by.

"Oh, good grief! Nick, we're moving!"

Six

"You hurt, missy?"

The voice was gruff and frightened.

Halley looked up into Archie's worried brown eyes. He was leaning down at the car window, shouting through the glass. The car was wedged firmly in the middle of a large clump of black raspberry bushes.

Halley shook her head and hunched over the wheel while she smoothed the front of her shirt. Was she dressed? Yes, of course she was. It was only in her imagination that she had shed all her clothes and dramatically professed her desire for the dark-eyed Baron. What was happening to her, anyway?

"We're fine, Archie," Nick confirmed loudly, opening his door to prove it.

"What happened?" Archie pulled Halley's door open and helped her out. "I was taking my evening constitutional when I heard this rustling sound coming through the thicket. Thought there was a trespasser and was about to go after him—"

"No." Halley shook her head and laughed shakily. "No trespassers in sight. Only Nick and me."

Archie slanted his head back and carefully looked her over down the length of his nose. His rough, square chin was set rigidly. "You sure you're all right, Finnegan? Your hair's all tangled and you have a mighty dazed look on your face like you might have hit the dash."

He reached out one broad hand and gently pushed a lock of hair from her eyes. "Any bumps?"

"Nope, no bumps, Archie."

Nick had walked around the car and draped his arm over her shoulder, and was making teasing taps on her neck. "We're both fine. Sorry I can't say the same about the raspberry bushes."

Archie shook his head. "Still doesn't make sense. Did someone run you off the road? Maybe we should call the cops. . . ."

Halley shook her head. The situation was bordering on slapstick comedy, and she no longer trusted her voice.

"What then? The brakes give out on you, Finnegan? Joe ought to take a look at that."

"He did," Halley managed to squeak out. "Just today. Brakes are fine, Arch."

Halley nudged Nick for not helping her out, but he only smiled, then tickled the skin on her shoulder.

Archie shook his head in total bewilderment. "Hell, you know, it's quite a scoop in the land here. I don't know if Nick and me are strong enough to hike her on outa there—"

"I think you're right, Archie," Nick said. "It'll be much easier in full daylight. Do you think Halley needs driving lessons?"

Halley glared at him.

Archie contemplated the question for a minute, then rubbed the stubble on his chin. "Don't know, don't know. It's the damnedest thing I ever saw. You don't know how it happened, huh?"

"Just one of those things," Halley murmured.

"One of those crazy things," Nick agreed.

While Archie looked on in sober amazement, Halley and Nick began to laugh, soft laughter that grew and grew until Archie began to laugh along, slapping his wide girth and throwing his head back. But he never did know why.

Halley slept soundly, her mind filled with rich, sensual dreams of Nick Harrington. His passionate kiss stayed with her, fueling her dreams, and his arms wrapped her tightly in an embrace she could still feel when she awoke the next day. When he showed up later that afternoon, it almost seemed to Halley as if he had never left.

"I came to help you get the car out," he explained, laughter lighting his smoky eyes. The heated air between them was electric and alive. After they'd freed the car and he was about to leave, he kissed her good-bye, and the kiss held for Halley all the substance of a passion that had been lit deep inside her and which grew each time he touched her.

There were no promises, no assurances that he'd be back, but each day Halley's heart waited while she went about the business of being a librarian, and almost every day he dropped back into her life for however brief a time.

Being with Nick filled Halley with a happiness she savored. He often lapsed into moody periods of quietude, but Halley told herself it was simply that he didn't get much chance to talk around her outgoing family and friends. She knew there was more to it, knew that there had to be reasons why he was uncomfortable sometimes, but he would tell her in time. Her suspicion that there was a lot more to Nick Harrington than his handsome demeanor revealed was all right too. As Scarlett would say, she'd think about that tomorrow.

•   •   •

"All right, Marian the librarian," Nick said, barging into her office the next Thursday morning. "Today is mine."

Halley looked up and her heart stopped. He did that to her now, easily confused her life functions, causing her heart to stop, her pulse to race. Her lips lifted in a smile.

He wore a pale blue-gray pair of slacks that fit him perfectly—loose enough to be decent, fitted enough to catch her eye and feed her imagination, not that it needed much help. The vee neck of his deep red cashmere sweater displayed a thatch of curling black hair that her fingers itched to touch. She quickly grabbed a pencil.

"Nick, hi! Today is . . . what?" She couldn't even concentrate on simple conversation!

"Mine. Today is mine." With determination he walked behind the desk and kissed her tenderly on the lips. The chair scooted crazily to the side, and Nick laughed and stopped it with one foot. "Halley, I've wandered around this place for days now—"

"Yes," she said softly. Was this it? she wondered. He'd finally realized where he was and decided to move on to a world more suited to Nicholas Harrington the third.

His fingers slipped beneath her hair and played with the soft, smooth skin of her neck. "And it's a damn nice place to be, granted, but do you realize how seldom I see you alone?"

She nodded slowly and wet her lips. It was true, of course. She had tried not to think much about being alone with Nick, because it sent her body directly into orbit.

"And it's driving me crazy! So today is mine. *All* mine. I'm taking you away from all these nice people that make up your life, and I'm going to have you all to myself for four whole hours."

"Nick, I—"

"Can go with you, and I'd love to." He kissed the top of her hair, but she felt the kiss somewhere deep down below her breasts. "That's what you're to say, my love."

"But the library—?" She tilted her head back to look into his face.

"Will exist without you, no matter what you think. You have a meeting later today—"

Halley's eyebrows lifted.

Nick merely smiled. "And between now and then you're free. Volunteers are handling the desk, and your fine, capable assistant, Kate, is in charge."

"You've—"

"—arranged all that. Yes. You see, I have this insatiable desire to see who Halley Finnegan is when she's not a contessa or a daughter or a sister or an aunt or a friend or a librarian. Now up, my love. We're wasting valuable time."

Halley stood and found that her legs were shaking. She placed one hand on Nick's arm, but when she looked up, she had no idea what to say.

"Speechless, I see." His eyes twinkled merrily, "Good."

Halley took a deep breath and smiled slowly. "I guess I'm not used to being swept off like this, Nick."

"That's all right. I'll make it worth your while."

When she laughed, her heart slowed to a manageable beat. "Where are we going?"

"We are going on a picnic, my love. Just you and me."

She looked at him questioningly and smiled. "And the food?"

"Waiting in my chariot." Before she could dig up any other questions or protests, Nick ushered her quickly out the door.

Halley hardly remembered the ride out of town, only that the windows were down and the fresh, sweet-smelling air of the countryside swirled around them. The silence was easy and comfortable, and she finally let go and allowed herself to sink into the delicious pleasure of having Nick Harrington there beside her. Alone.

"Here we are." Nick pulled off a one-lane road a short while later and parked the car in a small graveled parking area. "Ever been here?"

Halley looked around at the rolling hills and patches of thick woods that dotted the slopes. The trees were a flaming patchwork of color that took her breath away, and through the branches, off to the right, she could see the sparkling waters of a small lake. "No, I haven't, Nick. It's lovely!" She stepped out of the car and breathed in the pungent smells of earth and water and crisp autumn leaves.

"We used to ride horses around here as kids," Nick said as he opened the trunk and lifted out a woven picnic hamper. "Then they turned it into a park, but they have kept it fairly untouched. No hot-dog stands or boat houses."

Halley smiled and shoved her hands into the wide pockets of her skirt. She could picture Nick astride a fine, muscular steed, riding off across the hills, his black hair dramatic against the blue sky beyond.

Nick held the basket in one hand, tucked a plaid blanket beneath his arm, and led Halley over to a quiet green spot beneath a group of tall pine trees. It was utterly quiet except for the gentle lap of water along the shore in the distance and the slight breeze whistling through the treetops.

"This is perfect, Nick. A perfect spot, perfect planning. But what would you have done if it had rained?" She smiled up at him.

"When you plan something twelve hours ahead, you diminish your chances for error."

"I see. Then if something occurs without any planning at all . . . ?" Like himself, she thought, and the way he had fallen so unexpectedly into her life. Plop!

He'd landed right there in a world that made him oddly uncomfortable, and yet he kept coming back for more. What were the chances for error there?

"That remains to be seen." He smiled down at her, and she couldn't see behind the smile, nor tell if he had read her mind. "Hungry?"

"Starving."

He set the hamper down and spread the blanket beneath a tree. "*Voilà*," he said. "Now sit down and relax, my love. This is my show, and I want you to enjoy it completely."

With a sweeping gesture he lifted the hinged top of the hamper and pulled out a small silver bucket, two crystal wineglasses, and two gold-edged china plates.

"A picnic?" Halley stared in wonder at the items, then burst into delighted laughter. "Nick, this isn't a picnic, this is a carryout from L'Auberge!"

"I have to admit my expertise in the area of picnics leaves a little bit to be desired, but I think this should work okay." He shrugged boyishly, and Halley found herself touched by the uncharacteristic gesture. For a brief moment it wasn't the self-assured, suave Nick Harrington standing before her but a man who seemed strangely vulnerable.

He uncorked a bottle of Bordeaux and poured it, then handed a glass to Halley. "To picnics," he said, holding out his glass.

"To picnics," she answered. She sipped the wine, basking in enjoyment as Nick served. It was all so lovely, from the linen napkins, to the plates heaped with cold crab salad, to the hunks of crisp French bread and chilled fruit.

Nick set a silver knife and a fork on a filled plate and handed it to her, then took his own and stretched his legs out in front of him.

He leaned back against the thick, rough bark of the tree, letting the Indian-summer sun warm his face. He looked so relaxed here, away from everyone, Halley thought. So free and comfortable.

"You were right, Nick."

"Oh?"

"About coming here. It's wonderful. We do know each other as lots of different people, barons and contessas and librarians. Some are real, some aren't. And it's nice to get away from all that."

His hand covered her knee. "Agreed."

Halley brushed her hair behind her ear and looked at Nick intently. As much as she enjoyed being with him, she realized how little she really knew about him. She knew only the surface kinds of things, really, that and what her emotions told her.

His fingers curled around her leg and squeezed her playfully. "What do you think, my love?"

Halley was swept away by the tantalizing feeling and looked at him unflinchingly. "I think you've discovered a lot about me these past days."

Nick continued to rub her skin gently. "That, Halley Finnegan, is an understatement. Besides the more delicious things, such as the incredibly sensuous way you kiss, I've learned—"

"Seriously, Nick. You know me pretty much for what I am. Halley Finnegan, librarian. Large, openly affectionate family. Plain, ordinary childhood. Stubborn streak. Messy apartment. Crazy friends. I still know you as the Baron. Is that who you want me to know?"

He shrugged and continued to eat his salad.

"Well?"

"Well, what?" He looked at her, his deep eyes filled with teasing innocence.

"Nick! Sometimes you're exasperating." She wrapped her arms around her bent legs and rested her chin on her knees. "I want to know more about Nick Harrington. What kind of a kid you were. What mischief you got into. What kind of cookies your mother baked for you when you were nine. That sort of thing. You know, whether you ever skipped school—"

"Did you?"

"What?"

"Skip school."

She laughed, her gaze skimming the tops of the trees in the distance as she remembered. "Only once. All the students and teachers went to daily Mass before classes began, and one day Rosie and I were coming back from Holy Communion and we had the sudden urge to keep going, right out the back of church and down the street. We went to Pop's garage, and he took us out to lunch. Mom stayed mad at him for three days, a record for her." Halley took a bite of bread, then paused. "Damn you, Nick!"

He leaned his head to one side. "Halley, such an outburst! And from a librarian?"

"You've done it again." She narrowed her eyes and punched him lightly on the shoulder.

"Done what?"

"You switched things around on me. Now stop it! Listen to what I'm saying, Nick." Her voice sounded stern, but he found her smile enticing. "Tell me, did your mother ever get mad at your dad like mine did when I skipped school? Did you like college? What is your favorite book? Who was the most important person in your life while you were growing up?" She paused, then added teasingly, "And have you always hung around libraries for kicks?"

Nick slipped off her glasses and gently pressed one finger against her lips. "Shh. I once read that people who wear glasses don't talk as much if you remove them."

"Hah! An old wives' tale, if I ever heard one!"

There were sparks of irritation and amusement mixing together and lighting her eyes with starlike flecks of gold. Nick thought it was as lovely as any constellation he'd ever seen. "I see there is a touch of Irish temper beneath those gentle curves."

"Back to the subject—"

Nick considered her carefully. There were many things he already liked about Halley Finnegan. This was a new one that he hadn't considered before. She *did* want to know those things about him. She didn't care about his banks or his money or his *Mayflower* ancestors. She wanted to know who *he* was. It made him uncomfortable and touched his heart at the same time. But when he rubbed a finger along her cheek and began to answer, he was smiling.

"Okay, I give up. Yes, I skipped school. Lots of times. In all four of the boarding schools I went to. No, my dad never took me to lunch when I did it. I don't know if my parents argued; I never heard them if they did. One of my nannies baked me cookies; I don't remember what kind. Her name was Jessie, and she stayed with us the longest—nearly two years, I think."

"Nanny?" Halley asked softly.

Nick laughed at her expression. "Don't look so distraught. Some people are raised by mothers, some by nannies."

"Were they . . . nice?"

"Nice enough. Some more so than others. Ironsides was a bit of a burden, but she didn't last long."

Halley managed a smile at the triumphant look on his face, and she imagined a young Nick Harrington besting the nanny-dragon and sending her on her way.

"And your parents?"

"My parents were nice people, I think. I often wish I could have gotten to know them better. They raised me the best way they knew how, which was the way they were raised—sort of by remote control."

Halley's face had turned so utterly sad that Nick

inched over and put an arm around her for comfort. "It's all right, Halley. Really it is."

Halley looked up into his eyes and wanted to hug him—for several years, maybe—to fill in the hollows she was sure were there beneath that polished, strong front. "My family, Halley, was nothing like yours, but that doesn't make it good or bad. My folks both died when I was in college," he added, almost as an afterthought.

"That's why you're so close to Sylvia and Herb."

He nodded. "They assumed responsibility, although I was already an adult and didn't really need their help. I'm very fond of them." He drew Halley closer and whispered into the mass of silky hair pressing against his cheek. "And I'm very fond of you too."

"My family must overwhelm you," she said around the growing lump in her throat.

Nick leaned back again and sipped his wine. "I guess they do a little, at that. It's that informal, relaxed kind of loving they do that amazes me. Perhaps I don't understand it."

"What's to understand, Nick? Love is love. That's simply our way of showing it."

It *was* just that simple for her, Nick could see, but sometimes it wasn't really simple for him at all. He wasn't at all sure how to explain that to Halley, so he kept silent.

"Between nannies and now, Nick. Tell me about that time in your life." She nestled closer, and as she pressed against him, he stiffened slightly.

Nick looked off toward the hills, then rubbed his fingers up and down her back. His voice was low and hesitant. "Not much to tell, Halley. School, finance courses, and then the family banking business."

"I—I suppose a business like that can soak up years of your life," she said. He'd carefully put a distance there, stretched it out fine and firm between them. For a brief moment Halley felt sad and alone, but she quickly brushed the feeling away. *Nonsense, Finnegan,* she scolded herself. Sometimes she came on like a Mack truck. The man needed a little space, that was all, and the day was far too gorgeous to ruin because of fragile feelings. Smiling brightly, she lifted herself onto her knees and began folding napkins and piling up the plates. "You provided lunch, kind sir. I'll take care of the cleanup."

"Oh, no, you don't," he said, pulling her to her feet. "Leave it. We only have a short time left. Let's walk."

She smiled in agreement, eager to slip back into the comfortable closeness they'd shared earlier, and with their arms looped around each other's waists, they wandered through a nest of wildflowers and down the gentle bank to the lake. Their bodies touched with a new familiarity, and their minds were busy with the emotions that had gone unspoken but were weaving a gentle web around them. The distance may have been all in her mind, Halley decided. At least for now that's how she was determined to see it.

"It's so peaceful," she said, her head filled with the lovely day and her heart filled with Nick Harrington.

Nick nodded and pulled her closer, and he could feel her body warmth seep into him through his arms, his hips, everywhere their bodies touched. Her lush, ripe curves were a tantalizing delight just beneath his fingertips, and he felt he could walk forever like this. Just he and Halley, and brilliant splashes of sunshine showing them the way.

When they spoke, the conversation was light and pleasant, about things that didn't matter. It was enough that they were there together, hips rubbing gently and hearts reaching out.

When they circled the small lake and ended up

back at the picnic spot, they both felt inexplicably sad that they had to leave.

"We should have brought a Frisbee," Halley said.

"Next time," Nick said, knowing for certain he wanted there to be a next time.

They piled the china and crystal glasses and napkins back into the elegant hamper, and as Halley bent over to close it, she laughed out loud. "Oh, Nick—"

"Oh, Nick, what?"

"You left the price tag on your hamper."

Nick spotted the small white tag and tore it off the handle. "So much for impressing you with my casual, spontaneous picnic attempt." He lowered his head and kissed her lightly just above the ear. "The truth is out."

"But it *was* spontaneous—and very, very lovely." She lifted her palm to his cheek. "And I'm duly impressed, Nick. Thank you." Lifting herself on tiptoe, she kissed him slowly, loving being there with him, loving the day and the quiet of the park. It was Halley and Nick, and she no longer felt the awkwardness of the masquerade. Right now, for this special moment, nothing on earth mattered but the two of them.

Nick's hands lifted to nestle in her hair, and he moaned softly beneath her kiss.

"I'll go on a picnic with you any day," she whispered as she pulled away.

"Is that a promise?" Nick held her there for a long moment, his dark eyes asking for far more than picnics.

A familiar rush of warmth fanned out between her legs before burrowing down inside her. "Nick," she whispered softly, "is crab salad an aphrodisiac?" His husky laughter tickled her neck, and she pressed her cheek against his shoulder.

"Nope. It's you and me, that's all."

"Strange," she murmured.

"But very, very nice." He picked up the basket and led her to the car. They drove slowly back to town, the day a sweet memory between them.

"Halley," Nick said as they reached the stone gates to the Thorne Estate. "I have a bunch of business details to attend to tomorrow, and tomorrow night I want to see some friends who live a few miles away." Mostly he wanted to see Halley, but for reasons he couldn't quite come to grips with yet, he wanted to stop by to see the Melroses. *Needed* to do that. It was a new need, and it felt strangely comfortable and right. He strongly suspected that Halley was the reason he suddenly wanted to attend to his life connections, but he didn't wish to subject the whole thing to analysis. Not yet, anyway. He'd simply go with the feelings, spend more time out at the Melroses' place, and see what happened.

Halley nodded. "That's okay, Nick. I know you have a life beyond the walls of the Thorne Estate Library." She *knew* it but found it difficult to think about.

"Will you miss me?" He stopped the car at the bottom of the steps.

Halley blushed and pulled her glasses out of her purse.

"Why do you do that?"

"Do what?"

"Go for the glasses when you don't want to answer me."

She slipped them on and laughed lightly, then pushed down on the door handle. "Now that's not true at all, Nick. I fully intend to answer you. I just want to see you."

Nick reached over and held the door secure while he waited. His eyes sparkled with laughter. "Okay. Say it. Tell me you'll miss me."

Halley tilted her head to one side and smiled calmly.

"All right. Yes, I'll miss you. I've become very used to having you around, Nick Harrington, though I can't imagine why. So I'll miss you. There, I've said it." He was still holding on to her door, and his face was close to hers—close enough, she thought vaguely, to kiss if she was so inclined.

"That's it?"

"What do you mean, 'that's it'?"

"I mean, aren't you going to try to convince me to stop by, even for just a moment or two?"

Halley feigned an irritated expression. "No. I've survived a day without food before, I'm sure I can manage this somehow . . ." Her voice grew softer as she noticed a slight mist on her glasses.

His smile moved closer.

"Oh," she murmured.

"Mmmm," he said.

When his lips slanted hungrily across hers, and his hand heatedly caressed her cheek, Halley felt a rush of tender passion that convinced her, no matter what Nick said, that there *must* have been something in that crab salad.

Seven

Halley walked down the back steps of the library the next afternoon and watched the groups of parents and elderly citizens gathering around the gazebo. Friday. The busiest day of the week, and she was wandering around like a spoiled princess getting nothing done.

Nick might as well have come, she thought as she automatically picked up a piece of paper littering the ground and shoved it in her pocket. His presence was as real to her as he would have been if she could reach out and feel the wonderful, muscular bulk of him. It wasn't enough that she truly *did* miss seeing him. The images of Nick that filled her mind were confusing and passionate and disconnected and wonderful all at the same time. What *was* it about him that sent off warning signals? He was so right . . . and so wrong. Yin and yang. She had no idea why, but she knew one thing: It wasn't what was *said* that was causing the alarms but what *wasn't* said.

"Halley," Archie called from the gazebo, "it's time to proceed."

"Coming in a minute, Archie. Start without me

and I'll catch up," she called back, and hurried around the corner of the massive building to drop the wastepaper in the trash can. In her dazed state she'd almost forgotten that it was the last Friday of the month—Community Day. Archie planned special games for the young kids, which the older folks loved watching, and he always included some kind of a special treat. Today it was to be a lesson in gravestone rubbings out at the old cemetery, and she'd promised him she would show up for part of it.

"Hello."

Halley yelped like a frightened puppy and dropped the handful of paper to the ground.

"Halley, Halley." Nick held her gently by the shoulders. "I didn't take you for the nervous sort. It's only me."

"Nick," she managed feebly, a flush of embarrassment coating her neck. "I . . . well, it's a bit like seeing a ghost. Or having a thought suddenly jump out of your mind and look you in the eye—"

"You were thinking of me?" Pleased laughter spilled from his black eyes.

"You're not supposed to be here," she said, hedging.

"No, and I can only stay one hour. I forgot to ask you something yesterday, so I came by do to it today."

"It must be something momentous to require an hour," she said teasingly.

"Would you have dinner with me tomorrow night?"

His hands were still on her shoulders, and Halley felt the gentle heat of his touch begin to circle through her. "Dinner? That sounds very nice, Nick."

"Good. It's kind of a family affair. I'd like to show you off."

Halley gulped, then pulled off her glasses. "There's even more, isn't there? That's why you saved a whole hour to ask me—"

"No." Nick laughed, and when it rumbled up from

deep in his throat, Halley could feel it in her finger-tips. "Absolutely not. I saved an hour because I *have* an hour—wedged in between work and visiting the Melroses—and there's nowhere I'd rather spend my hour than right here with you."

Halley smiled softly. "Oh. Well, that's nice, Nick." Beyond his shoulder she spotted Archie's group heading for the cemetery. "But as much as I'd like to, I can't, Nick. I promised Archie . . ." She pointed toward the group of people disappearing beyond the rise in the distance.

"No problem. I'll come too. It wouldn't be my first choice of places to spend a valued sixty minutes with you, but I'll settle for what I can get."

His arm went around her shoulder naturally, and just as naturally Halley lifted her hand and wound her fingers lightly in his where they rested near her neck. "Lead the way," he whispered into the loose strands of her hair that rubbed against his cheek.

They headed across the yard at a leisurely pace, intending to catch up but reluctant to hurry.

"What's up with Archie?" Nick asked as they walked beneath the tangled branches of ancient elm trees.

"Archie is about to give the Friday Community Club—which is a loose assortment of people between the ages of five and eighty-five who happen to be free on the last Friday of each month—a lesson in gravestone rubbing."

"Hmm." Nick considered her words. "The only rubbing I can imagine, Halley, is something I'd like to do with you."

Halley swung her hip playfully into his. "This is serious business, Harrington. Shape up now."

"May I wait until we get there?" His fingers slipped from hers and walked down across the slight rise of her breast.

"Nick!" Halley said, but no reprimand found its way into the hushed exclamation.

The clipped rhythm of small feet running across crisp leaves separated them in an instant.

"Well, hi, Mickey!" Halley said, brushing her hair off her cheek and calming the fleet of unleashed butterflies in her stomach.

The small boy ran up and happily wedged himself between them. "I'm late, Aunt Halley. You too! Hi, Nick," he added shyly.

"Hello, Mickey," Nick said.

The youngster grinned up at Nick, then reached instinctively for his hand.

Halley watched curiously. At first Nick looked surprised, then uncomfortable. Mickey didn't notice and simply grinned and tugged Nick's arm until he could grasp firmly on to his fingers. Then he bounced along contentedly beside him. When Halley finally caught Nick's eye, all she could detect were dwindling traces of the passion Mickey had dampened so quickly, and the odd uncomfortableness. Well, she thought as she smiled regretfully at him, so her Baron wasn't very used to children. Most bachelors probably weren't. It took exposure, that's all.

"Mickey is explaining gravestone rubbings to me," he said solemnly over the sandy curls covering the youngster's head. Halley nodded, and they walked toward the group of people gathered around Archie in the small cemetery.

Nick was still ill at ease, Halley could see. "Mickey's an expert at this," Halley said.

"It seems like a strange pastime," Nick answered.

They walked up to the edge of the crowd, and when Mickey left them to crouch down in the front row, Halley looped her arm through Nick's and squeezed his hand. "Nice to have you back again," she whispered in the brief second before Archie hushed them all and began his short lecture.

"This is Whisper Cloud's grave," Archie explained carefully and thoughtfully, so the kids wouldn't miss a word, "She was a brave Indian maid who lived many, many years ago." He pointed to the dates on the gravestone.

As Nick and Halley listened, the kindly hobo retold the tale of the young girl and how she courageously left her family to travel many, many miles through a devastating winter to bring back medicine for the tribe.

Then he showed them how to place their paper on the letters of the gravestone and rub with the lead until the words appeared in relief.

"Mr. Harrington will try it first." Archie swept the air with his hand, motioning for Nick to step up to the gravestone.

Nick was startled at first, then walked toward Archie, looking, Halley thought, as if he were afraid to step on something he shouldn't. When he reached the gravestone, he seemed reluctant to touch it. She stood still, watching the incongruous scene: the tall, handsome man whose strength was visible in his very stance, hesitant to participate in the children's exercise. Then, for just a fraction of a second, she saw pain in his eyes.

Halley was stunned.

"We rub with even pressure," Archie explained in a gravelly voice, and the moment passed.

"You did very well," she said, smiling up at Nick when he returned to her side.

"I'm a quick learner." He returned the smile, and Halley breathed easily again. Perhaps it had been her imagination playing tricks on her.

They passed from grave to grave, with Archie filling the youngsters' minds with wonderful, colorful stories, and they in turn carefully rubbed meaningful epitaphs off the gravestones to take home with them where they'd retell the stories to brothers and sisters and parents.

"How does he know so much?" Nick asked.

Halley grinned proudly. "The Thorne Estate Library reading room. He's a smart man, and living here where he can nourish his mind sure beats skid row."

Nick thought about that for a minute, and then, as the group started to walk back to the library, he held Halley back with a quick, sudden hug.

She smiled. "What's that for?"

"Things. Things you do. And are."

Halley slipped her hand into his and walked on. They kept several yards behind the others, close enough to hear, far enough to be lost in their own world.

"Well," Halley said as they approached the gazebo, "I guess you have to go."

Nick glanced at his watch. "I have twenty-seven minutes left. Are you trying to get rid of me?" He traced a finger along the lovely rise of her cheekbone. He couldn't remember when minutes started being so important to him, but he knew it was a recent phenomenon. Minutes were things to get through, to savor, but now Halley had him counting minutes and seconds, and each one with her was becoming more and more special.

"Of course I don't. But—"

"Hey, you two!' Mickey yelled as he skidded to a stop at Nick's feet. "Wanna have a sack race with us?"

Halley pulled away quickly.

"A sack race?" Nick asked.

"Yeah, it's great!" Mickey assured him. "It's the last activity for the Friday Club. Aunt Halley?"

"We'll see. Run along, Mick," Halley said with a smile.

"Sack race?" Nick furrowed his brow and swung her hand lightly.

"Well, it's kind of a tradition," Halley reluctantly explained. "The kids like it when I join in with someone as my partner. They like to beat me is what they like to do," she said with a laugh.

"What do we do?"

"Well, the partners get in a sack together—"

Nick's eyes lit up, and he laughed with enthusiasm. "Now you're talking! Count me in."

"A potato sack! And mind your manners, Mr. Harrington. I'm ticklish!"

The raggedy line of contestants was already formed when they got there, two small, wiggling bodies in each huge burlap sack. Archie ceremoniously handed them the last one. "Here you are. Now we shall see which generation is more adept."

"Hah!" Halley said, and climbed in beside Nick. "We accept the challenge."

They drew the rough fabric up around their waists and tied it firmly, while Archie fashioned two fingers into a mighty whistle that Joe Finnegan always claimed he could hear clear over in his shop.

"Ladies and gentlemen, on your marks," he bellowed loudly.

"I think I'm going to like this," Nick whispered into Halley's ear.

"How could you have gotten through childhood without sack races?" Halley asked, trying to ignore the tight press of his thigh against hers.

"How I got through puberty without you is more the question."

"Nick, get your mind on the right track!"

"In the sack, you mean?"

Halley groaned.

"Get set," Archie intoned, and when he brought his fingers to his lips and blew gustily into the clear air, the race began in earnest.

Mickey and his partner took an early lead, followed closely by the seven other youthful sack racers, while Halley and Nick attempted their first hop. "Come on, Nick, together now!" Halley shouted above the noise of the laughing kids and the senior citizens and parents who had settled on the grass to watch.

Finally Nick got the hang of it, and the two hopped sluggishly across the lawn. "Hey, I think I could get good at this!" Nick yelled breathlessly. The feel of her body pulled close to him was wonderful; he reveled in having her hips and the long length of her leg pressed against him. He looked ahead and saw the line of kids turning around at the edge of a wooded area and heading back to the finish line. Nick picked up a little speed.

"Hey, my legs are shorter, don't forget," Halley yelled, her mind blurring as their limbs rubbed against one another again and again.

"But spectacular just the same," replied Nick with a sensuous grin. "Come on, Contessa, they're passing us on their way back!"

It was when they got ready to turn around that they took the tumble. Halley felt it coming first.

"Nick!" she screamed, her arms flying out in front of her as a mighty hop brought them just to the edge of the woods.

Their legs were one tangled mess, and when she opened her eyes, Nick's face was an inch from hers. He was smiling.

"These sack races aren't bad at all."

Halley tried to move, but it only brought her body into closer contact with his. She felt hot all over. "How . . . how do we get out of this?" The clean, sweet smell of leaves and matted grass drifted around them. Beneath her, Nick's head was cradled in a puddle of sunshine.

"I'm rather enjoying it." Nick's hands moved into her hair, his fingers threading through the tangled waves.

"Nick . . . the kids . . ." she murmured in the tiny sliver of space between their faces.

"Are long gone, my love."

Halley lifted her head an inch and looked beyond the trees, over the wide expanse of green grass. In the distance she could hear the shouts of childish laughter as the children joined their parents and said their good-byes to Archie.

"They've given us up for losers, I'm afraid," Nick said with no trace of remorse in his voice.

"Losers, hmm?" Halley felt dreamy and wonderful. Gravity had pressed her whole length against him, and she could feel all of him keenly, ankle to ankle, thigh to thigh, belly to belly.

"You're so beautiful, Halley."

"You make me feel that way," she answered simply. She smiled as he drew her head down and kissed the tip of her nose, then each cheek, her eyelids, and finally captured her smile completely with his full and loving kiss.

"Do you suppose we could stay here forever?" Halley asked when she finally pulled her head up for a needed breath of air.

"And they'll find us millions of years hence, like a piece of petrified wood," Nick said, his thumbs caressing her cheeks. "Woodland creatures twined together—"

"—in a potato sack! What an interesting cultural exploration we'll start." She laughed, feeling bubbly with happiness and tingly with the excitement of Nick lying beneath her. She felt hot all over and it was becoming more difficult to breathe, but she couldn't seem to get herself to move.

"The Sack Era." Nick kissed her again, long and passionately, then squirmed beneath her body.

"I'm too heavy for you," Halley said quickly, and slipped over to the side.

"It's not that."

"What, then?" When she looked into his eyes, she knew the answer before he spoke, and bit softly on her lip. It wasn't only she who was hanging on to restraint by a thin thread.

"There's just so much a man can take . . . you understand?"

Halley began wiggling out of the sack. "Of course. Women aren't so terribly different, you know." Her heart was beating quickly. Petrified wood, bosh! Lying on top of Nick Harrington had released a million fireflies that spread their flickering light to every nerve ending in her entire body.

"Smokey the Bear would be proud of us," Nick said, but his voice was strained with emotion. He pulled the sack from around their ankles and helped Halley to her feet.

"For putting out the forest fire?" She smiled shakily and reached for Nick's arm.

Nick nodded.

"I guess we should go back." Halley brushed the leaves and twigs off Nick's sweater. "You have to leave."

"I guess I do. We seem to have a terrible problem with timing, Halley."

"Well, maybe we'll get better with practice," she said huskily.

"No doubt." Nick filled his lungs with air and willed his body to calm itself.

The sweet-smelling breeze drifted through the woods and gently massaged their backs as they walked slowly along the path. It was easier to breathe up here, Nick decided absently, but then, everything was easier here. Walking and talking and moving through time. The unplanned days had a richness to them that his hectic, jammed-packed schedule hadn't allowed for. But that was the kind of life he'd wanted since Anne died, wasn't it? Busy, propelled, filled with activities to keep his attention shifting from one thing to another. Diversionary tactics.

The kind of simple peace here was something he'd

wanted to steer clear of. Stillness allowed thoughts to balloon into life and emotions to rage.

Then why wasn't he raging?

Hell, who was he kidding? No, it wasn't really the place at all. It was Halley Finnegan. *She* was the simpleness, the beauty he felt, the peace that was making him feel loose and comfortable.

Their hands, fingers entwined, swung lightly as they walked, and Nick Harrington began to hum.

Beside him, Halley smiled.

Eight

Halley slept in short spurts that night—starts and stops that her mother used to call "angel naps."

"*Devil* naps would be more like it," she mumbled as she groped her way to the small kitchen shortly before dawn to fix herself a glass of milk.

She had thought that by this time Nick would be on his way, with the wind at his back. And she'd be the wind, she and the Thorne Estate Library and the very plain life she lived, pushing him away by their very ordinariness. He was still around, though, and Halley was finding it more and more difficult to imagine it any other way.

She took the hot milk off the stove and poured it into a mug Rosie had given her that read, "Good friends hang together." It had a picture painted on it of two shirts hanging on a clothesline, arms around each other.

She stared at it for a minute, then hugged her robe to her slender body and walked to the window shaking her head. "No, Finnegan, just who are you trying to kid, anyway? These aren't friend-type feelings you feel toward your Baron. These are feelings you've never felt toward *anyone*." She sipped the hot milk and looked out the curtained window toward the huge golden moon that seemed to be hanging just above the library. The rest of the sky was inky black, with only a single star dotting the galaxy.

"Star light, star bright . . ." she said dreamily, as the milk took its toll.

Miles across the city in a penthouse apartment that would hold Halley's cottage in its bosom and hardly know it was there, another sleepless dreamer watched the moon and the single star.

"I wish I may, I wish I might . . ." Nick murmured as he took another drink of Scotch. "Might what? Might go to bed with my Irish Contessa and love her through the dawn." He took another drink. "Might sweep her off on a mighty steed and conquer the world . . . might settle down with her in a vine-covered cottage . . ."

He slipped one hand into the silky sash of his robe and leaned against the French door that led to his rooftop patio. "Might . . ." His mind was groggy, but it wasn't the drink; he'd had only one. It was Halley Finnegan who was blurring his mind, drugging him. Slowly he returned to his wide bed and removed his robe. It was his Contessa who was haunting his dreams, and the dreams were no longer enough.

". . . get the wish I wish tonight." Halley closed her eyes tightly to make a wish. But what would it be? That she might have an affair with Nick Harrington, ex-baron, rich man, banker? Or a life with Nick the wonderful? A week? A day . . . Her eyelids drooped. Or a dream about the two of them together, twined as tightly as a vine . . .

She smiled groggily as she set down the mug and padded off to bed. "Good night, my Baron," she murmured into her pillow, then fell asleep with a lovely smile on her face.

When she awoke in the morning, Halley grimaced against the morning light. Angel naps didn't make one feel very angelic. Nor rested, she decided tiredly.

She showered, put on a soft, forest-green warm-up suit, and gulped down a glass of milk, half expecting to hear Nick's knock at the door.

He had gone off the previous day without mentioning their "date" again. Maybe, she thought hopefully, the family deal had fallen through and she could talk him into a candlelit pizza dinner for two. Or maybe . . . maybe there wasn't to be a date tonight. The last thought caused a swift sadness to pass through her.

The ringing of the phone was a welcome sound in a room that suddenly felt too quiet.

"Rosie, hi!"

"Halley, you sound too pleased to hear from me. What's wrong?"

"Nothing, you dope. I *am* glad to hear from you."

"I thought I'd start your day off right by telling you mine started out with a real treat. . . ."

Halley slipped down into the chair beside the phone and curled up her legs beneath her. One never knew how long Rosie's tales would take.

"I ran downtown to the Hyatt Towers early today to deliver some dresses for an ultra-fancy affair being held there tonight—"

"That's great, Rosie! Business must be booming."

"Wait! That's not the treat. As I was leaving, just whom should I spot crossing the lobby but . . ."

Rosie paused for dramatic effect, and Halley groaned. "On with it, Rosie!"

"Baron Nicholas, the Hunk, that's who!"

"Nick . . ."

"Aha! I can tell by the way you say his name, Halley, that soft, sexy sound . . . there's more going on here than an exploration of the Dewey decimal system! Oh, Finnegan, I hope—"

"Rosie, stop."

"You like him a lot, Halley. I can tell from your voice and the wonderful look in your eyes these days." Rosie's voice had lowered to a steady, caring tone. "We haven't been friends from toddlerhood for nothing, Finnegan. I know. I know he's different from the other men who've moved in and out of your life . . ."

"Okay, I *do* like him, Rosie, a lot. But—"

"But you're worlds apart. Who the hell cares, Finnegan? You can hold a candle to *anyone*."

"But it's not just that, Rosie. Sometimes I feel I only know a tiny part of Nick, and that's what I've become enchanted with. Its the unknown that scares me—"

"Then get to know him better! Heavens, Halley, there are plenty of women who would covet that job!"

"Oh, Rosie, you *do* have a way of simplifying things—"

"I happen to think love is simple, Halley." Rosie's voice was strangely calm. "It's only we complicated folks who tend to muck it up sometimes. Don't, Halley."

"Rosie, you are ridiculous! Who said we're talking love here?"

"Whatever we're talking, Finnegan, it is right and good. Incidentally, the way you say his name is *nothing* compared to the way he says yours!"

Halley laughed softly. "Oh, Rosie, you're the eternal romantic. Was Nick alone?"

"Nope. He was with a delightful woman."

Halley felt a quick stab of disappointment, then shoved it aside quickly. "Oh?"

"Yes, a lovely gray-haired lady whom he calls Aunt Syl. You've met, he says."

Halley tried not to notice the feeling of relief she felt. "Yes, Syl was the mystery-party hostess. She *is* lovely. Nick is quite close to her."

"Well, Halley, I've got to scoot. We're having a sale today. Come by if you can. Ciao."

" 'Bye, Rosie." Halley hung up the phone and picked up her Saturday list of things to do, but her energy for routine things seemed to have disappeared. She wanted to curl up in a chair and . . . and what? And nothing. How silly of her.

She ran a brush through her hair, grabbed her list, and allowed herself only a minute to stare at the phone.

Were they having dinner tonight or not? An edge of discomfort crept into her thoughts. Damn, it was happening. This wasn't a dream any longer. Dreams you woke up from and went on your merry way, holding in the good feelings, tossing out the bad. You didn't stare at phones and wish them to ring, or expect *him* to come strolling down your walk in the middle of the morning.

Halley sighed, grabbed her glasses from the table beside the door, and hurried out.

"I'm bringing a date tonight, Syl." Breakfast was finished, and much of the usual chitchat was behind them. Nick had had an early-morning meeting at the bank, and when Syl suggested breakfast afterward, it seemed like a good thing to do. He hadn't seen her since the mystery weekend.

"Darling, that's fine. You know you're always welcome to bring someone." Sylvia Harrington lowered her coffee cup and smiled affectionately at Nick. "Is it someone I know?"

"Yes and no." He motioned to the waiter for more coffee and then continued. "It's Halley Finnegan."

"Halley Finnegan . . ." Sylvia tilted her head to one side thoughtfully. "I don't believe I know any Finnegans, although the name has a vaguely familiar ring to it."

"Halley was my date at your party. The Contessa."

"The Contessa, of course! Leo Thorne's friend."

"Yes, and now she's my friend too."

Syl studied him for a moment. She was silent.

"I've seen her a few times since then—"

"She is certainly a ravishingly beautiful woman."

Nick leaned back in the chair and rested his hands on the white linen tablecloth. A small smile eased the tension in his jaw. "The Contessa is, yes. Halley is beautiful, too, but in a different way. It's hard to explain, but you'll see."

"Nicky, I can see from your eyes that you are very fond of Halley Finnegan."

He nodded. "At first she was a lark, a mystery woman who beckoned me into the vast unknown. You know, an exciting fling. I wanted to follow her, discover her."

"And . . . ?"

"And I may have discovered far more than I can handle. The feelings that she . . ." He lifted the bill from the silver tray and smiled at Sylvia. "I don't know, Syl. It's definitely not the lark I was expecting." His eyes seemed to deepen as he thought about her, and the smile lingered. "She's far more like a nightingale, you might say."

After paying the waiter Nick helped his aunt from her chair, and together they walked out into the restaurant lobby, unaware of admiring glances at the handsome picture they presented—the elderly gray-haired lady with the demeanor of a queen and the handsome younger man at her side.

Sylvia touched one gloved finger to her cheek thoughtfully. "You know, of course, that Abbie and Stan will be with us tonight, Nicholas."

Of course he did. It hadn't been a conscious decision to bring Halley, just a vague feeling that the Melroses should meet her again. Maybe things would make more sense then. Maybe set against the backdrop of his life connections he'd see things more clearly.

Nick straightened his tie automatically and picked up his car keys from the marble-topped table beside the door. Time to go. When he'd finally reached Halley on the telephone in the late afternoon, he told her he'd be by at seven-thirty, plenty of time for them to drive downtown to meet the others. She'd thought that sounded fine and hadn't even asked who "the others" were. It was a simple kind of trust that left him feeling strangely protective toward her.

The drive to the Hill was becoming second nature to him; he felt he could close his eyes and the car would find its way to Halley, wherever she was, and the thought made him vaguely warm and content.

After Anne had died, he hadn't immediately decided not to get involved again. It was simply that that kind of energy had been sucked out of him the day he buried her. He'd lost his connection to things that mattered, and he had found a way to function quite nicely within a framework of frantic work; extravagant, whirlwind vacations; and indifference. The indifference made everything bearable. There'd been plenty of women in his life and that had worked just fine. Until now.

Without reducing his speed, Nick made a sharp right turn into the Thorne Estate.

Hell, what was he doing thinking such serious

thoughts? They'd known each other such a short time. She knew so little about him. So *damnably* little . . .

Halley was ready and on her way out to the car before he stopped the engine. "Anxious?" He laughed as he opened the door and helped her in.

"Just ready. And happy to see you."

Nick sat still for a moment, taking in the sight of her. She was lit by moonlight, and her hair was alive with an unearthly red-gold shimmer. It seemed fuller tonight, waving down like a gentle waterfall until it reached her shoulders.

"Do I look all right? Since I didn't know where we were going, I took a chance." He was staring at her with an expression that filled her with longing, and she had to pull her gaze away from his.

"Perfect," he murmured, and started the engine. No, *perfect* wasn't the right word, but he didn't want to wait around to find it, or they might never make it to the club. She wasn't the Contessa tonight; she was Halley Finnegan, in all her tender, natural beauty.

The eyeglasses she usually wore had been replaced by contact lenses, and they made her blink in an appealing, sexy way. Her dress was an emerald-green silk that heightened the light in her eyes. Its simple scooped neckline was broken only by a small cameo pin in the center.

Nick didn't think it possible that he could be so moved by loveliness, but it took an heroic effort not to ditch the whole evening's plans and drive directly back to his apartment. He rubbed the back of his fingers lightly against her cheek and fiercely fought his desire, finally dropping his hand to the wheel and pulling the car onto the main road.

"Well, Nick, just where are we headed?" Halley asked lightly, feeling acutely that one of them needed to neutralize the air in the small car—and the sooner, the better!

"The River Club. Syl and Herb have a sort of tradition. We get together at the club once a month, and that assures we stay in touch."

"The three of you?"

"No." Nick pulled the car onto the highway and headed downtown. "There's another couple. You may remember them from the party— Abbie and Stan Melrose. They're close friends."

"That's nice." Halley directed her attention out the window at the flickering lights passing by and tried to place the Melroses, but she couldn't. She'd met so many people that weekend. Well, it didn't really matter. She'd meet them soon. The Harringtons, the Melroses, Nick. She wondered briefly why he had called it a family gathering but let it pass. Friends can be almost family; Rosie certainly was.

The River Club was a luxurious club in downtown Philadelphia. It sat on top of a hill that commanded a breathtaking view of the city and the river below. Nick was greeted familiarly by the tuxedoed maître d', and then they were led to a linen-draped table beside a wall of windows where Nick's aunt and uncle welcomed them warmly.

Halley immediately felt comfortable with Syl and Herb, just as she had at their home, and wondered briefly what Nick's parents had been like. They must have been quite the opposite of these two lovely people, whom she couldn't imagine ever giving their child to servants to raise. She'd tried to tell her sister Bridget about Nick's upbringing, but as Bridget's brood milled around them, Halley had found herself unable to. Although Nick was matter-of-fact about his past, she found this particular aspect of it nearly impossible to comprehend, and the nagging, uncomfortable suspicion that there was more to tell grew right along with the depth of her emotions.

"Ah, here they are!" Herb rose from his chair, and the other three at the table followed his gaze.

A couple, slightly older than the Harringtons and both elegantly dressed and distinguished-looking, joined them.

When the introductions were made, Halley did remember meeting the Melroses. She realized Stan had been the one who'd solved the murder, and she'd sat next to Abbie at dinner and had thought her charming and lovely. When she watched Nick seat the gray-haired lady next to him, she remembered something else—the deep affection for the older woman that Nick had shown, even when acting as the Baron von Bluster.

The Harringtons had perfected the art of entertaining, and Halley found herself carried along on the lively conversation and superb dinner. But all through the creamed oyster appetizer and the delicate veal in wine sauce entrée, through the fine glasses of expertly chosen wine, she was intensely aware of Abbie Melrose and the careful, attentive way she listened to every word that came out of Halley's mouth.

"Have you lived in this area all your life?" Abbie asked as they dipped into the creamiest chocolate mousse Halley had every tasted.

"Yes," Halley answered with a smile. "Except when I went away to college, but there's a bit of the homing pigeon in me. I came back to stay."

"You're a librarian, Nick says." She said it kindly, as if she thought it was somehow a delightful thing.

"Of sorts," Halley said, then launched into an animated description of her duties at the Thorne Estate Library. "It's a wonderful job for me," she finally concluded. "I love kids, books, and mayhem. This job gives me incredible doses of all three." Her face was flushed, and she hoped they all understood it was from her enthusiasm over her chosen career and didn't suspect that Nick's fingers were creating havoc with her composure beneath the table.

No one seemed to notice.

"Leo is a friend of all of ours and says wonderful things about the library," Herb said, leaning back in his chair and allowing the waiter to light his cigar. "But mostly he says wonderful things about you, Halley."

Halley smiled and dipped her spoon back into the mousse. She wasn't learning nearly as much about these people as she would have liked. Perhaps it was time she directed the conversation.

"Enough about me. Mr. and Mrs. Melrose, tell me, how long have you known Nick?"

Abbie Melrose seemed startled by the question. She looked briefly at Nick, then back to Halley, softening the look on her face with a smile. "We've known Nick since he was a little boy. His parents were acquaintances, and Nick spent many hours in our home."

Each word seemed carefully chosen, although not insincere. Halley looked carefully at Stan and Abbie and decided to ask Nick more about them later. Her question seemed to have bred slight discomfort in them which she didn't want to heighten.

Sylvia then picked up the conversation and enthralled them all with stories about a recent trip she and Herb had taken to Australia.

Halley listened, smiled, nodded, and felt perfectly at ease. Except when she felt Abbie's gaze gently trying to read her face.

"Well, folks," Nick announced as he noticed the tiredness in the older couples' eyes. He stood and pulled out Halley's chair. "I think I'd better get my librarian home. She's not much of a late-nighter."

Abbie looked up at Halley and and took her hand between her own lined palms. "Halley, this has been a delightful evening. Stan and I would love to have you come out to our home sometime to visit." She looked briefly at Nick, then back to Halley. "Do have Nick bring you out."

Halley pondered the invitation as they waited for the valet to bring the car. It hadn't been exactly an invitation. It was more a statement of something that should be done. Strange. Yet it had been done in a most warm, gracious way. Halley was puzzled, but just as she was about to say something to Nick, the car arrived beneath the canopied entrance to the River Club.

"They're lovely people, Nick," Halley said as they drove out of the circular drive.

"Yes, they are. So are you." One arm reached over and slipped around her shoulder.

It felt good, and Halley realized that although she'd felt at ease, there had been a tension to the evening.

When Nick pulled her closer, she laughed lightly. "These little cars don't allow much getaway room, do they?" She tugged lightly at the fingers nesting in the hollow of her neck.

"Do you want to get away?" he asked.

She didn't answer right away, as if she were putting a tremendous amount of thought into it, but she really didn't need to think at all. She had wanted to enter Nick's world to put some perspective on her feelings, but it hadn't helped. She wanted Nick terribly, and right now it didn't matter where he came from or where he was going or if he'd been raised as a Russian czar. She curled her fingers around his and lifted them to her lips. "No, I don't want to get away."

His fingers began to work magic on her neck muscles, and Halley made a small contented noise.

Nick smiled. "If you're not too tired, how about coming to my apartment for a nightcap?"

She nodded against the curve of his arm and let

his warmth seep into her. She'd known he'd ask; she'd known she'd say yes. . . .

Nick's apartment was in a tall modern building only minutes away. A glass elevator whisked them up to the top floor, and Halley was grateful that Nick's arm had remained around her waist the whole time. She didn't trust her knees, and it might have alarmed the other couple who rode with them as far as the eighth floor if she melted into a puddle at their feet.

As soon as the wide, polished doors opened on the top floor, Nick turned her toward him and kissed her hard until her knees did give out. It didn't matter, because Nick's arms were tight around her.

"I couldn't wait one more second."

"Chocolate mousse . . . and now this," Halley murmured.

"Which is better?" Nick nuzzled little kisses into her hair.

"Hard to say, Harrington. They're both sinfully delicious."

The heat from his kisses passed through her like an electric current, and every tiny part of her was touched and sparked to life.

"Nick . . ."

He finally pulled away. "Yes, my love?"

"My contact fell out."

"Halley, you say the most romantic things." He looked into her eyes but didn't notice the absence of the lens. Both eyes looked devastatingly beautiful.

"It might be on me," she said softly, trying to examine the front of her dress without moving.

"Ah, let me handle that." With sure fingers Nick explored the front of her dress, pulling out the silky material from her hips, then lazily circling the neckline. "Don't see it here."

His voice had turned husky, and the searching,

sliding movements were turning her mind to mush. She took in a quick little breath, and Nick responded immediately to the lift of her breasts.

"Ah, maybe there!" his fingers slipped beneath the edge of the material and rubbed along the creamy peach rise of her breasts, back and forth, then dipped a fraction of an inch to explore the lacy top of her camisole. "Now, it could be . . ." Two fingers slipped between her breasts and moved slowly up and down, sliding over the silky skin.

"Oh, Nick," Halley murmured.

"I haven't found the contact yet."

"You've found plenty of contact. I can barely breathe. May we go inside?"

Nick's fingers did one more curling, tantalizing search of her breasts, then moved upward. "Certainly. The search-and-find maneuvers were a success."

He cupped his hand and showed her the tiny contact lens in the center of his palm.

"I won't ask when, in said maneuver, it was found."

"Good idea," he murmured. "But if it gets lost again, at least I'll know the territory."

Nick unlocked the mahogany double doors and ushered her into a small, elegant entry hall.

"Please aim me toward the rest room, kind Baron, and I shall restore my sight."

Halley was back in seconds and found Nick in a spacious living area pouring two glasses of sherry. His back was to her, and she took that minute to look around the room. Nick's apartment. It had been in her dreams, of course, but it hadn't looked anything like this.

The room was exquisitely decorated. Heavy glass-topped tables sat beside curved, upholstered chairs; chrome étagères were positioned against the silk fabric walls and displayed statues, golden eggs, and

carved glass animals that caught the light and reflected it back. There was a marble fireplace without
any ash in it, shiny and clean. Everything was perfect.

Nick turned around and smiled when he saw her.
"Well, this is it, home sweet home." He moved to her
side and handed her a crystal glass.

Halley walked slowly across the thick mauve carpet, taking in the brass-edged liquor cabinet and
the perfectly placed art books on the coffee table.

Nick followed close behind. Finally he drew her
down onto the cream-colored sofa. "Well, do you like
it?" There was laughter in his voice.

Halley wet her bottom lip.

"The apartment, I mean."

When she finally met his glance, she saw the laughter spilling out. He knew she didn't like it. Of course
he did. He'd been living in her world too long not to
know that. "Well, it's certainly elegant . . . and perfect . . ."

"And . . . ?" Nick nudged.

Halley tilted her head and scanned the room.
"Well . . ."

"Out with it, Halley." Nick's arm curled around
her neck.

Halley offered him a half smile. "It looks like a
room that took itself too seriously."

His deep laughter filled the room. The penthouse
meant nothing to him. It was a place to sleep, to
entertain if need be. It wasn't a home and never had
been. "Too serious, huh? That's terrific, Halley. Well,
someone had to take it seriously. I sure as hell never
have."

"No offense to your decorator."

"Now, how did you know I had a decorator?" he
said, teasing.

"There isn't one inch of the Nick I've come to
know in this room."

"Not one inch?" He took her hand and rubbed it across his lap.

Halley coughed. "Well, perhaps that needs to be amended."

"To . . . ?"

He held her hand tightly against his thigh, and Halley could feel the hard, hot skin beneath his pants. "To six or so feet of the Nick I know. The rest of the room belongs to a stranger." Halley looked sideways at his wonderful profile and left her hand exactly where he had put it. In just a few minutes they would be finished talking about the decorating scheme of his apartment, and then there would be nothing left except what was flooding both their consciousnesses. This lavish space now held a man and a woman who were only aware of each other. Nothing else existed anymore.

"Well, I guess that's enough decorating talk," Nick said huskily.

"I think so."

He swallowed hard. "Halley, you might not know me as well as— "

She leaned her head sideways until she looked directly into his eyes. They were smoky black, and deeper than the blackness of the sky beyond the window. They were compelling and filled with desire. "Nick, I know that. I suspect there are huge chunks of your life that I don't know anything about, and that scares me sometimes, but what I do know is quite wonderful. I don't know how you landed in my life, or why, but with you I feel a whole new kind of happiness—"

Nick could barely speak. Every nerve in his body was fighting to explode. It wasn't just desire, although heaven knew that was shaking him to the core, but it was *feeling*, honest-to-God caring about this woman who was turning his life upside down.

He didn't just want sex with her, he wanted to *love* her in every way possible.

"Halley, I want to make love to you."

"I told you I wasn't looking for a getaway."

"I can't believe I'm saying this." His fingers dug up beneath the loose thickness of her hair. "I want you so desperately that I can hardly control myself, but I want you to want me too."

Halley fought the huge, welling rush of emotion inside her. She thought she would choke or drown if it reached the surface. Finally, from somewhere in the back of her throat, a voice whispered, "Nick, I want us to make love as much as you do."

Nine

The light was out in the bedroom, and neither of them made any move to turn it on. Halley could see everything she could possibly want to see.

Moonlight collected in a fine pool on the wide brass bed, and the rest of the room was in shadow. Nick led her through it, one arm draped around her waist.

Classical guitar music played softly in the background, although Halley didn't remember hearing it in the other room. Suddenly she felt different, each sense alerted, awakened to everything around her: the muted light of the moon resting in lazy patterns across the bed; the sweet, musky smell of the man beside her; the whistling rustle of a breeze through an open crack in a nearby window. At the edge of the high bed, Nick stopped and stepped away from her slightly, turning her until she was lit with soft moon glow.

"I want to look at you for a moment," he whispered, his hands slipping down her bare arms. "You're so very, very beautiful, Halley."

Halley's heart lurched. Nick's eyes were filled not only with desire, but also with a tenderness that touched her profoundly, and she couldn't speak.

When she reached up to touch his face, he took her fingers instead and held them to his lips, kissing each one separately, then pressing them to his mouth. She was a gift, a wonderful goddess who was sent to him, and he wanted to savor every single moment with her. He wanted to know every tiny inch of her, every desire. But most of all, he wanted to please her immensely.

"Nick," she said in a low tone, a small smile lifting her lips and dimpling one cheek, "why do you suppose we're whispering?"

He laughed into the palm of her hand, and it sent tantalizing tickles down her arm. "I don't know. I know we're not in church. Maybe it's because I'm standing here touching the most sensual librarian in the world." He let her hand drop to her side and rested his palms on her shoulders, warming them on the velvety softness of her skin. "There's something forbidden about that."

"Being sensual? Or touching a librarian?" Her arms circled his waist, and she hooked her thumbs into the waistband of his pants.

Nick lifted one hand up into her hair, and the locks slipped like silken threads through his fingers. "Hmm, I'm not sure. Certainly librarians aren't forbidden." He kissed the tip of her ear. "Nor things sensual—as a concept, anyway." While he dropped tiny kisses along the side of her neck, his hands slowly circled Halley's back. "But *sensual librarians,* I think that's the key here."

Halley's head fell back beneath the stirring vibrations caused by his knees. "I think sensual is something you are only with another who makes you that way."

"Is that so?" Nick slowly unbuttoned the back of her dress.

Halley could only manage a nod.

With sure movements he gently pushed the dress

off her shoulders and down the smooth curve of her hips, letting it fall in a green puddle at her feet. He stood perfectly still, memorizing the way she looked at that moment, so fresh, so unassuming, so lovely. She was all silk and cream, the lacy camisole and panties melting into the supple smoothness of her skin. Hungrily he loved her with his eyes.

Sensual, Halley thought dreamily. Whatever the feeling was, it was attacking her in rippling waves between her legs and spreading like a forest fire along her skin! She moistened her lips and looked up at Nick's handsome face. "And you, my dashing Baron, you definitely know how to make me feel sensual."

Nick's husky laugh fueled her desire, and bravely she spread her fingers beneath his waistband, relishing the lovely feel of his bare skin. "You may be releasing a demon in me, who knows?" she said teasingly.

"I could become addicted to demons. . . ." His hands spread wide and traveled up and down her sides, exploring each small hill of her ribs, then the luscious curve of her hips. His fingers played on her thighs, burning wavy patterns into the firm skin. "Oh, Halley, Halley," he said, then groaned, his hands suddenly leaving her body and tugging at his shirt.

Halley helped him, her nimble fingers plucking buttons out of holes and pushing the crisp white material off his torso. The whole time, her eyes caressed his face and recorded the warmth and desire that poured from the deepest part of his eyes. "I've always thought the name Halley was rather plain, like calico," she murmured into the heated air between them. "But you say it so magically, it makes me think of satin and silk instead."

"Believe me, you're satin and silk—" His fingers toyed with the lacy edge of the camisole only a second before he slipped the tiny straps down over her shoulders. Her breasts spilled free and glistened, high and round and lovely in the hazy light of the moon.

His sharp intake of breath stirred Halley, and she felt the quiver of desire swell within her.

Slowly Nick took one breast in the broad palm of his hand, pushing upward against the curve as gently as the touch of an angel's wing. His thumb circled the darkened center, and he felt it harden beneath his touch. Tiny ripples of excitement pushed outward from her skin and set fire to his fingers.

"My Contessa with the magic freckles," he murmured, then bent his head to taste the golden flecks scattered across her skin.

"No one . . . no one has ever kissed my freckles before," she said with difficulty.

"Good. Now they are mine alone to cherish." His tongue made slow, easy movements on her flesh, and Halley felt her limbs weaken.

"Nick . . . I'm going to fold up . . . right here . . ."

With a sure sweep, one arm curving beneath her buttocks and the other cradling her back, he lifted her and laid her carefully on his bed. She was as light as a feather in his arms, a wisp of a woman who was filling him with an almost painful kind of joy.

"Better, my love?"

She nodded. Everything was better. It was the best, the floating, free feeling, the sure feeling that Nicholas Harrington III was about to make love to her . . . and the overwhelming desire that she wanted him to, every bit as much as he did.

"Nick, my wonderful Baron." She lifted her palms and placed them flat against his bare chest. It was broad and shadowed with thick, dark hair that felt rough beneath her touch. Halley twisted her fingers into it, then rubbed back and forth across the springy curls, delighting in the heartbeat that pounded beneath her touch.

Her eyes lifted to his. The smoky desire that met her look seeped into her, and she knew the fires that they'd left smoldering for so many days were not going to be put out this time.

In seconds Nick had stripped off his pants and the rest of Halley's clothing and was stretched out beside her on the wide bed, his weight on his hip and elbow as he gazed down into her eyes and stroked her hair lovingly.

Halley watched him as his gaze traveled over her, across her breasts, then slowly down her body, all the way to her feet, and then back up again. Everywhere his eyes paused, a resting fire stormed to life beneath her skin, until she felt her whole body bathed in thick, sweet flames.

"How . . . how lonely it must be for you in this huge bed." She touched one finger to his face and slowly traced across the strong cheekbone, curling one knee toward him.

Nick nodded slowly. He never knew how lonely it was until now, and he wondered vaguely if he'd ever find sleep in it again without this magical dream of a woman beside him. "Sometimes. But not anymore. You've done something to me, my little Irish temptress, made me feel something again." Her hair was spread out on the pillow like a peacock's tail, and he scooped up a handful of it and pressed it to his cheek. I don't want that feeling ever to go away."

"I'm feeling a few things myself," she answered, her finger running across his lips and his jawline, then down the taut cords in his neck. "I can't seem to keep my hands off you, Nick." Her palm moved lower and began rubbing lazy circles across the naked skin of his stomach. She felt no awkward newness with him, no jitters, no embarrassment, and the thought brought a tender smile to her lips. It was as if she had known him before and they had found each other again. "Maybe we *were* together, my Baron, some other time."

"In some other life, maybe? Who knows?" He kissed her hair and ran his fingers down the column of her neck. "How well do you suppose we knew each other then?" His hand cupped her breast and began to massage it gently to the rhythm of his words. "This well?"

The amazing pleasure of his hands on her skin rose up inside her, and she quivered.

"You're like a lovely bird—unafraid, soft, and fluttering." Her response to his touch filled him with an incredible warmth, and Nick moved from one breast to the other, rubbing, squeezing gently, pressing her nipples between the pads of his thumb and finger until they grew hard and firm. He could feel her blossoming, opening up, and his hand slipped lower, sliding across her stomach, then her abdomen, in slow, easy movements.

Halley closed her eyes and gave in to the wonder of his touch. When his fingers slipped down to her thighs and played their magic back and forth, she felt such an explosive welling up of love that she bit her bottom lip until it nearly bled. "Nick," she said with a gasp. "Oh, Nick, you are turning me into a mass of jelly."

"The loveliest I've ever tasted," he said as he dipped his dark head and began a dance with his tongue on the rise of her breasts.

Halley drew her arms around his neck and dug her fingers into his thick hair.

"I want to know every inch of you, Halley—" His head bent again, and his tongue found one of the hard nipples waiting for his kisses. He circled it slowly with his tongue, licking and sucking and loving the taste of her, unable to get enough. Was it possible to get enough? He couldn't imagine ever not wanting Halley with the utter intensity that filled him at that precise moment. It was a life-giving intensity, and without it he felt he would surely die.

His breath was hot on her breast when he spoke. "Halley, I've needed you for so long, and I never even knew it. . . ." He lifted one of her hands and held it flat against his chest, then slowly lowered it down the hard span of his body.

"No, let me," she whispered, and continued the journey with her hand.

Nick groaned at the lightness of her touch, heavenly caresses that nearly drove him wild. "Oh, Halley, you do know how to bring out the beast in me."

She leaned toward him, pushing her breasts into the wall of his chest, all the while her fingers gently squeezing him to the brink of ecstasy. "The beastly Baron is a very gentle soul beneath it all. A kitten, that's what."

"Only with you," he growled, the meaning of his words no longer important. Every word, every letter, was a love sound, and it all meant the same. His arms went around her then, and he lowered her back against the pillows. When he leaned over, his face just above hers, his eyes were filled with such startling intensity, Halley could barely speak.

"Nick," she said raggedly. "Nick, I—"

"Shh." His lips came down in a crushing kiss that took her breath away. His tongue plummeted deep into the velvety cave of her mouth and flooded all the tiny spots inside her. He stroked the inside of her mouth, loving her, wanting her, until it stopped his breath completely and he had to pull away for air. "Halley," he murmured into the thick, hot space between them.

Halley's fingers were tunneled into his hair, and her eyes were open wide, watching every etched line in his face, every movement of his jaw. "Yes, Nick. I want you." She spoke so softly, he almost didn't hear her, but he read her lips, and his words blended with hers so that neither was sure who spoke. It didn't matter.

Then, with a desperation he could no longer control, Nick eased himself on top of her. Parting her thighs, he positioned himself between them and, with what little restraint he could muster, slipped gently into her.

The arching of her back was instinctive, a welcoming movement that forced him deeper inside her.

"Oh, Nick, I want you so." Her arms wound around him tightly, her hips pressing into him. She couldn't seem to get close enough. She wanted to be totally one, meshed so completely together that this searing joy would never leave her.

Her eyes closed as the room began to fade, and all that was left were she and Nick, wound together and transported on tiny pads of air toward golden shafts of light somewhere in the distance.

She felt him moving inside her, smooth and hard and warm, and felt her body tighten around him. Then the floodgates of pleasure tore open, and she clutched at his back as they soared off into the sky. His deep growl of total joy reached out for her. She answered, and then they slowly tumbled back to earth, wrapped together in a primal, rocking peace.

Halley walked quietly out of the bedroom with Nick's thick robe wrapped around her. It touched the ground and was large and cumbersome around her waist. When she rubbed her cheek against the wide collar, she could smell Nick in the velvety fabric. It smelled wonderful.

A small smile on her face, she headed for the kitchen. She hadn't seen one the night before but assumed that even Nick Harrington's apartment would have a kitchen, and she found it beyond the spacious, perfect living room.

She walked through a splash of yellow sunshine

on the polished tiled floor and stopped short. How could she be so calm and normal? She, Halley Finnegan, had just spent the night with Nick Harrington. No, not *the* night. She had just spent one of the loveliest nights of her life with Nick Harrington. No, she had just *made love* with Nick Harrington. Several times, in fact. Several *wonderful, lovely, tender* times.

What had awakened her an hour ago as the sun began to creep up the eastern sky was the awareness that she had not only made love with Nick Harrington but *loved* him as well.

And that was a whole new kettle of fish, as Joe Finnegan would say.

Halley walked over to the cupboard and rummaged around until she found a tea bag, neatly stashed in a labeled canister.

Of all the unlikely men to fall in love with, Nick won first prize.

In love with . . . Halley pondered the words as she filled a teakettle she found beneath the shiny stove and put it on to boil. What exactly did that mean, anyway? She'd never tried to analyze it before. She walked over to the window, waiting for the kettle to whistle. Outside, the day was just beginning. *A beginning . . .* Maybe that's what all this was about. She felt new and reborn, and all those things you read about and saw in the movies.

It had crept up on her, this feeling. Each time she was with Nick, it was fueled, and when she slept, her dreams had nourished it even more. And now . . . and now she had loved him completely. Yet deep down, she knew she was only beginning to know Nick. He was so many different people, and there might be more she didn't know about yet. But all her mind could attend to for any length of time was the fact that Nick had somehow become an integral part of her.

Halley answered the call of the kettle and poured the water into a mug. She sipped her tea thoughtfully, then padded her way back through the living room. She looked at the room once more in the clean light of day, but it was the same: elegant, tasteful, expensive, and cold, without any personal trace of the man who was filling her with such joy. There were no pictures, no books with curled pages, no slippers peeking out from beneath a chair or sofa.

She pulled the robe more tightly around her and hurried into the cavernous bedroom. Curling up in a chair beside the bed, she cradled the warm mug in her hands. Tiny shafts of sunlight spilled across Nick's face as he slept, and she watched the shadows playing with the angles and bones of his face. His mouth moved every now and then, sometimes lifting in the beginnings of a smile; sometimes parting slightly, then closing again. Halley watched, fascinated. There was enough right there in his face, she decided with a small smile, to absorb her attention for a lifetime.

Nick stirred.

"Hi," she said softly.

His lids opened slowly. "I must have died and gone to heaven."

"Uh-huh. Me too. Would you like some tea?"

"No." One well-muscled arm came out from under the silky sheets and reached toward her. "I want you."

Halley set the cup on the table and moved onto the bed, sitting down next to him until her hip pressed cozily against his. She looked at his tousled black hair and smiled.

Nick shifted beneath the covers.

"It's morning, Nick. Would you like something to eat? I'm starved."

"Eat?" His fingers crawled into her lap, and slipped beneath the voluminous folds of the robe.

"Food, you know." She squirmed as the heat of arousal spread through her.

"Let me just hold you first." He withdrew his hand and tugged her down beside him, wrapping his arms around her tightly and cradling her head to his chest. "I need to be sure you're real, Halley."

She nodded and rubbed her cheek against his bare chest.

"I don't want to ruin the night with words, but I do want you to know this—"

She tilted her head up until she could see the tenderness and love in his eyes.

"—it was very special, Halley, even more than I dreamed it would be."

The sensations that flooded through her were too overwhelming to describe, so Halley nodded again. Why did she feel tears building up? This was a happy time. . . .

Nick twisted his fingers into her hair and kissed her gently on the forehead. "I didn't expect this to happen," he murmured softly into her hair.

"Nor I. Barons and librarians don't usually end up in bed together."

"It's a pity. It works so well."

Halley laughed. "Shall we try to reeducate people?"

"I'm a selfish man, Halley. I only care about us." He stroked her gently while he talked, his fingers rubbing across the fleecy fabric of the robe. "You've filled a big void in me that I wasn't planning on having filled."

"What kind of void, Nick?" Her voice was just a whisper, and the words were ones she somehow knew he wanted to hear.

"I was married once, Halley, to a wonderful woman. Her name was Anne Melrose, and she died in an automobile accident. . . ." He paused while Halley digested his statement and made the necessary connections. Damn, he should have told her this days ago, but he hadn't expected to care so much. . . .

Halley's heart lurched. Her mind grabbed on to the words and processed them neatly, but her heart refused to stop clamoring beneath the thin wall of her chest. "Melrose . . ." she murmured.

He drew her closer. "Yes, she was Abbie and Stan's daughter."

"You loved her very much."

He nodded against her hair. "Yes. She was the . . . the first person in my life that I loved." He had always, in his thoughts, said *only* person he had loved. Halley's presence had changed that, and Nick stirred, feeling vaguely guilty. "And she loved me back, fully, without any reservations or calculations. When she died, a part of me was buried too. I didn't think I'd ever be able to love again."

Halley thought of the cemetery and the shadowed pain she had seen on his face. "It must have been awful for you."

"I moved into this condo and built a life of work—"

"—and parties," Halley added.

"A foolish kind of escape, but one I knew well." He kissed her cheek. He wanted to make love to her again, right away, to block out the old, painful memories, but he couldn't. His feelings for her were too important. Loving Halley was complete in itself; it couldn't be connected to any other purpose. He eased himself away from her and pushed back the covers. "Maybe we do need some food."

Halley lay still while he walked across the room, her heart full of a range of feelings that defied categories. She watched his naked back and loved the way he moved, bending over to pull the shade, stretching in the thin light that slid through. She hated to think of the hurt he'd been filled with.

And she had trouble imagining a woman other than herself in his life.

By the time she'd showered, Nick had a stack of lukewarm toast piled in a basket on the kitchen table and was struggling to release two flat, anemic-looking eggs from the skillet. His thick hair was combed, and he wore a pair of blue jeans with an elegant blue cashmere sweater.

"Jeans. I've never seen you in jeans before," she joked, padding across the floor in bare feet. Her thick hair hung loose and free about her shoulders, and she wore a huge yellow warm-up suit that Nick had pulled out of his closet. "Sexy. Very sexy." She slapped his buttocks playfully.

"Careful there, Contessa. Little do you know the power of your touch."

Halley wrapped her arms tightly around his waist while he put the eggs onto the plates. "When will you admit I'm not a contessa?" She loosened her arms and moved alongside him. "There's no contessalike glamour here, Nick. Finnegan glamour, maybe—that's all." She wondered briefly what Anne had been like. Her mother was certainly elegant . . .

Nick slipped his fingers beneath the fall of hair and kissed her lightly on the top of her head. "What kind of glamour is that, my love?"

Her voice was soft and husky when she leaned her head back to look at him. "Oh, Pop says it's a little auto grease or garden dirt beneath your fingernails now and then, and a sparkle in your eye. That's about it."

Nick felt it again, that crazy, earthquake-type lurch, only it came from inside him, not somewhere under the ground. He reached down and captured her fingers between his palms, his voice strangely choked. "How much more glamour could a man handle? Now eat, Halley, or you'll blow away."

They sat across from each other at the glass-topped kitchen table, plates of eggs, the aura of their love-making, and thoughts of Anne Melrose Harrington between them.

"You may have to use your imagination with this breakfast. I don't cook much," Nick apologized.

"It's fine." The eggs slid down her throat, and she watched Nick's hands as they held the fork. Strong, firm, wonderful hands. "How long ago?"

"Four years."

"That's a long time, Nick," she said softly.

He reached out and held her hand tightly, pressing it into the thickly woven table mat. "Time kind of stopped. It's hard to explain, Halley. Our lives have been so different, yours and mine. Your family . . ."

"My family?"

"The way they dish up love so readily—big daily doses of love. Mine was different. I never even knew my parents, really, and with Anne I felt that kind of closeness that you've probably never *not* felt. It gave me a footing. And when she was gone, it was too. I couldn't seem to get things together."

"I see." Halley threaded her fingers through his and lifted his hands to her lips. A lot of things fell into place now. Not everything, but certainly more. Beneath the handsome, powerful facade of her Baron was not only a loving, kind man, but a vulnerable one as well.

Nick watched her closely. He wasn't sure what she was thinking; hell, he wasn't even sure what *he* was thinking, or why he had gone into all of this. Why was he thinking of Halley in terms of his future when she had so recently become a part of his present? He looked out the window at a perfect, blue sky, but it held no answers.

A pleasant sensation drew his eyes back across the table. Halley's head was bent so that her hair flowed over his fingers in rippling auburn waves, and slowly, carefully, she was kissing the pad of each finger on his hand.

"Nick?" she murmured softly.

"I'm right here," he said, his voice suddenly dropping.

"I have an hour and a half before I said I'd meet my folks for Mass. . . ."

"An hour?" he said vaguely. "And a half . . ."

"We could do the dishes or . . ."

He nodded. Hot, fiery streaks were shooting from his fingers to every imaginable part of him.

While he was thinking, Halley walked around the table and coaxed her way onto his lap, pulling his arms around her.

". . . or we could make more eggs."

Nick moved his legs beneath her in delicious torment. "Or?"

"Or we could watch an hour and a half of a two-hour movie." She wiggled and sunk deeper as his legs parted slightly.

"Or we could . . ." He slipped his hand beneath the warm-up top and began to stroke her stomach lightly.

"Mr. Harrington the Third, where is your mind?" she said huskily.

"Let's see if we can find it," he breathed into the hollow of her neck. "If I can still walk. That may be a problem by now."

Halley slid off his lap. "I'm sure we can take care of whatever the problem is." She glanced down at his bulging jeans and grinned mischievously. "We're down to one hour and twenty-eight minutes."

"And we're not going to lose another second." Nick grabbed her hand and led her back into the bedroom.

Ten

Nick tossed and turned in the bed. It *was* lonely without her, lonely as hell.

He stumbled into the kitchen and plugged in the coffeepot. He wanted Halley Finnegan beside him, wanted to twist his fingers tightly into her thick, silky hair and have her head tilt back, her eyes look up at him, a sea of love and laughter cascade over him.

He had loved her. He loved her. Yes, it was love. Nothing else could account for the way he felt. He also knew, because Halley was incapable of shrouding anything in those lovely green eyes, that she loved him back.

Nick slid open the terrace doors and stepped outside into the crisp breeze that blew over the city. Traffic was starting to get heavy, people were moving down below, tiny insectlike figures on the sidewalks and streets. He breathed in the air deeply, trying to block out the parts of his mind that were shouting at him, warning him that when you loved someone, you let them know all of you and what you were all about. Otherwise, they only loved part of you, and what would happen when they discovered the rest?

Nick shook his head and walked back inside. He'd think about it later. Maybe when he met Halley for lunch. Maybe tomorrow.

"You're beautiful." Nick kissed her lightly, and then once again, not so lightly.

"And you're clouding my glasses." Halley took his hand in hers and fell in step beside him as they walked down the street. "Rosie's meeting us. She invited herself to lunch."

"Where?"

"Finnegans' Place."

"Your folks?"

"Yes. Why pay when you can get it free?" She laughed, bouncing her hip against his. "Besides, my mother was feeling cheated. Everyone had met my incredibly sexy friend but her."

Nick watched the light reflect off her hair and breathed in the clean smell of her. She'd suggested they meet outside the neighborhood post office today, and that had been fine with Nick. He'd meet her anywhere she said, and he'd go to a doughnut stand with her for lunch if that's where she wanted. Or Pierre's in France. Or her mother's.

"I'm having a hard time concentrating on my library work, Nick," she confessed solemnly.

"What?" He tried to focus on her words instead of the gentle sway of her body against his.

"Work. You—you're becoming a liability."

"Hmm." He leaned down and dropped a flutter of kisses into her hair. "What are we going to do about that?"

Halley squeezed his hand tighter. "Don't know. I can't seem to walk past D. H. Lawrence's books—or Balzac's—without this crazy sensation carrying me off."

"It sounds serious." Nick released her grip on his

fingers and wrapped his arm tightly around her. "Maybe I could camp out in your closet. Then we could—you know—take care of problems as they arose."

"Librarian Finnegan's closet . . . hmm. I think I like the sound of it."

Nick slipped one hand inside her red cardigan sweater and lightly began to rub the soft jersey material of her shirt. "What about the feel of it . . . ?"

"Nick!" Halley blushed fiercely but made no move to pull away. "You now have sent at least three shop-keepers to the phone, and *if* it reaches the postman, by dinnertime everyone will know Halley Finnegan was molested on River Street by a rogue with black hair and sex-starved eyes." They turned off the business street onto a block of neatly kept two-story houses.

"Sex-starved eyes?" Nick laughed huskily.

"Well," Halley said demurely, "I know mine are, so I assumed the same about yours."

"There is certainly a bit of Irish fire beneath that calm, easygoing exterior."

"Aye." Halley nodded. "And it's off to the back of me soul with it for now, because here we are." With a sweep of her hand she motioned toward the white two-story house off to the right. Clumps of neatly pruned red-and-gold marigold bushes dotted the walk-way leading up to it, and stretched across the front was a wide, freshly painted porch.

Nick smiled and started up the sidewalk. "Some-day, Halley, I'm going to get me a porch just like this."

"A porch." The thought made her smile. Nick, who had everything money could buy, including a high-rise apartment, wanted a porch—a very *middle-class* porch. "It might be difficult to attach it to the side of that building of yours."

"Maybe I'm outgrowing that building," he mur-mured, surprised by the passing thought.

"Why do you want a porch, Nick?"

"I don't know. I think maybe it's because porches are for sitting on, and talking and laughing, being close. It's an image I've had tucked away since childhood."

"Like vine-covered cottages," she said, weaving her fingers through his and thinking hard about porches.

The screen door swung open as they reached the top step. "Hello! You must be Nick." A small woman with Halley's eyes stepped out onto the porch and captured Nick's hand.

"Hello, Mrs. Finnegan," Nick said as he looked down into the familiar sea of green.

She smiled. "Jane, please."

Nick scrutinized her face to find Halley's features in it. Except for the eyes, he couldn't, but her face was very lovely just the same, outlined by soft brown waves of hair wisping around her high cheekbones.

Jane turned and embraced her daughter, then ushered them both inside. "Rosie and Mickey are stirring the soup." She wiped her hands on her apron, and they followed her through the small hallway into an enormous, warm kitchen..

"Hi!" Rosie looked over her shoulder, her eyes sparkling. "Make yourself at home."

"Thanks, Rosie," Halley retorted. "Don't mind if we do." She walked across the waxed wooden floor and sat down on an old-fashioned oak bench with a high back. Nick joined her, his gaze sweeping the room. The bench was in front of a huge brick fireplace, and on either side were two cushioned chairs. Everything was within earshot of the large working island where Rosie and Mickey were diligently stirring.

Nick glanced at Mickey, who was lifting a large spoon to his lips. "Say, sport, seems everywhere I go, I see you."

Halley's head jerked up to stare at Nick. For a

moment she wasn't sure why she was surprised, and then it came into focus. It was his tone of voice . . . or the lightness to his words. Or something. He'd greeted Mickey with a new ease that she was sure had not been there before, and it pleased her far more than was rational.

"I knew you were coming," Mickey said, his huge blue eyes watching Nick. "And Grams likes me to be here."

Jane Finnegan laughed, and Nick discovered something else Halley had inherited from this lovely lady— that soft, lilting laugh with the silver edge to it. "Mickey is our little pass-around," Jane continued, "since he's not in school full-time. And he does love my Irish stew."

Mickey walked over and nudged his way onto the bench beside Nick. He looked up and smiled, and Nick smiled in return; then, without thinking, he settled his arm around the small boy's shoulder.

"Seems you have a little fan in our Mickey, Nick."

Nick smiled and gave Mickey a playful rub on the top of his head, then settled back and watched Jane glide around the kitchen, pulling down bowls, folding napkins without a thought, straightening a marigold leaning against the vase. Halley had gotten up to help her, and the two of them moved in an unspoken rhythm with each other, laughing at small things the other said, teasing Rosie as she tasted more than she stirred. He caught Jane watching Halley, paying close attention to the shining, lovely glow that touched her smile. He wondered what she was thinking, how she felt about it. Halley looked like he did, like someone alive with the glow of loving.

Suddenly Jane dropped her dish towel on the counter and walked over to the table where Halley was straightening the place mats. "I love you, little Finn," she said as she hugged her daughter tightly.

Nick felt the power of the exchange all the way

across the room, and it caused him to shift involuntarily on the bench. It was intimate—and so natural.

Jane looked over at him and smiled. "Halley was our firstborn, you see, and her father was so proud of her, he took her everywhere: Knights of Columbus meetings, parades, restaurants; and she was nearly a fixture at Finn's garage. Folks took to calling her little Finn, a chip off the old block." She brushed Halley's hair back from her forehead and laughed. "Although she's far prettier than Joe."

There it was again, that easy loving manner. Nick cringed slightly, wondering if it was something he could learn.

During lunch Rosie regaled them all with tales of searching through an attic in a Gothic mansion for dresses for her store and accidentally locking herself in. The old lady who owned the house forgot she was there and was sure it was a ghost making all the racket, so she had found a mystic and held a seance in the drawing room.

Halley watched Nick as his strong face softened in amusement. He seemed oddly comfortable in this room that had held years of laughter and tears and loving.

They left the house after lunch and walked back to the post office, reluctant to go their separate ways. "I feel like a kid," Halley murmured. "I have a pile of work a mile high, and all I want to do is . . ."

"Is?" Nick curled his fingers around her shoulder and played with her hair.

"Is be with you and figure out these past few days. No, I take that back. I'm not sure I want to figure them out. I simply want to find a way to make them last, to freeze the moments."

"Things don't ever stay the same, Halley," Nick said. "But that doesn't mean the future can't be good."

"Doesn't it?"

Nick didn't answer. He just pulled her close and walked on. Lord, she felt so good and so right in his arms. Loving her felt so right. Would he lose her? He didn't think he could bear that. Not again.

His hold tightened until finally Halley wiggled beneath his fingers. "My Baron is certainly strong."

He loosened his grip immediately, and his voice was rough. "I'm sorry, Halley. Did I hurt you?"

She shook her head and calmed him with a tiny smile. "I was trying to read the pressure of your fingers. I thought maybe you were sending me a message in code."

"Maybe I was."

She stopped walking and turned toward him. "What was it?"

He stared at her. Her rust-colored hair was blowing slightly in the breeze and was outlined majestically by sunlight. Her breasts bounced slightly beneath the jersey, and her smile tugged at something so deep inside him that he found it difficult to speak for a moment.

"Nick?" she asked softly.

His fingers played with her waist. His eyes sought hers. He didn't think he'd ever say the words again, but then he hadn't in his wildest moments dreamed that a Halley Finnegan existed for him. "I love you, Halley. I don't have any right to, but I love you."

"Does one achieve a right to love? A license?" She lifted her hands to his shoulders, and her chin tipped upward. "I love you, too, my Baron. Very much."

Her eyes closed as his lips met hers, but Nick's remained open, absorbing every small detail of her.

Halley pulled away, and when she spoke, her voice was husky with feeling. "And now the postman can say the handsome rogue was molested by that brazen Irish hussy, Halley Finnegan. And we'll be even."

They walked to their cars and parted, the words between them already taking on a shape of their own. They'd said it, "I love you," and now what? Halley wondered as she sat still in her car and watched Nick drive off. It was like a third party, a presence between them that they'd given life to, allowed to be. What would it do, now that it was?

"Halley," Nick said the next day, "I'm sorry to do this, but I'm not going to be able to come to dinner as I promised."

His voice sounded tired, Halley thought. Is that what "I love you" does? Tires you out and makes you break dates? "All right, Nick—"

"I'm sorry, my love, I want very much to see you, but . . ." He paused as if he wanted Halley to fill in the gaps and tell him why he couldn't see her.

"I understand, Nick. But I will miss you."

Miss you. The words screamed at Nick. That didn't begin to explain the way he felt. His whole body ached for her, needed her to soothe it, make it whole again. She'd given life to parts of him that were dead, and they needed constant, second-by-second nourishment. Nick pressed one hand against his temples and tried to stop the throbbing. "I . . . I'll call you tomorrow. I love you, Halley."

He replaced the phone and checked his watch. It was still early afternoon. He'd take the whole day, try to put his life in order. Could he put his life in order in a day?

Within an hour he was on the highway, headed toward the country. The sky was a deep violet with only a smattering of clouds that looked like cotton stretched across a painted landscape. When he looked up at it, he could almost hear Halley humming and see the sparkle in her eyes that the beauty of the sky would light there.

Stan and Abbie Melrose's estate was vast and sat alone at the top of a rise in the forested countryside.

He'd always loved it out there. He and Anne used to ride bareback through the woods for hours and hours, but now, when he drove by, the image of Anne didn't shout at him and tear him apart; it merely was, and he wondered if Halley liked horses.

Anne. She would have wanted him to love again; he knew that. She'd even like Halley, although their worlds would never have brought them together. She wouldn't have wanted the devastation that filled him, absorbed him completely, when she died, but he hadn't been able to help it.

He parked the car at the edge of the drive and walked up the familiar steps that had become a pattern in his life. Stan was coming out of the library when he walked into the spacious entry hall.

"Nick, good to see you." He glanced at the grandfather clock in the corner. "Earlier than usual, but that's good, very good. You know, we're both thrilled you're managing to drop in a bit more frequently these days." He smiled warmly and led the way into the living room. "Abbie's been resting, but she'll be down presently."

"Is she ill?"

"Old age, Nicky, my boy. It happens to the best of us, I'm afraid."

Nick looked long into Stan's lined eyes. They were aging, he and Abbie, and he hadn't allowed himself to see it.

"Nicky!" Abbie Melrose slowly walked into the elegant living room, her eyes lighting up at the sight of him.

Nick was at her side in a second and kissed her cheek affectionately.

"Before you say one single word, I want to set a date with you."

"Sure, Abbie, what gives?"

"I want you to bring Halley out, Nick. I *very* much want you to."

Nick sat down on a brocade sofa and leaned his arms on his knees, his eyes focused on the swirl of color edging the Oriental rug in front of the fireplace. "You do, do you?"

"Yes, Nick."

"I can't fool you, can I, Abbie? Never could. You know exactly how I feel about her, don't you?"

"I don't know about the 'exactly,' Nick, but I could hazard a guess. I like her very much. She's natural and sweet and kind. And she obviously loves you."

Nick managed a half smile.

"And you love her . . ." Abbie Melrose's voice was thin, but there was a strength behind her words.

Nick saw the emotion expressed in her face, and he felt it fill the air.

Nick nodded. "How about if I bring her out next weekend?"

Footsteps in the hallway caught the attention of all three adults, and they looked toward the door as a large woman in a gray dress filled the space.

"Nanny Jenkins, you're right on time," Abbie said pleasantly.

"Ma'am, Mr. Melrose, Mr. Harrington." She nodded politely to each person, then stepped aside for her charge to enter.

A small girl dressed in a pretty sailor dress and tights, her black hair flowing down her straight back and her eyes large and luminous, walked slowly into the room.

"Nell—" Nick started to rise, but the little girl politely walked over to him instead. She placed one hand on his knee, lifted herself on tiptoe, and carefully placed a kiss on his cheek.

"Hello, Father."

Eleven

"Hello, Nell." Nick reached for her and pulled her up onto his lap.

Abbie smiled over at her granddaughter. "It's a beautiful day, Nell. What would you like to do with your daddy?" She was looking more and more like Nick, Abbie thought, with those dark, smoky eyes and thick black hair. But she had her mother's lovely skin, a tea-room complexion, smooth like fine porcelain. She was a beautiful little girl, and Abbie's heart swelled with love every time she looked at her.

Nell smiled. "Horses?"

She was so shy around Nick, it pained Abbie, but it was understandable. She hardly knew him. That pained Abbie even more. Nell needed a father, and Abbie wondered how much longer it would take for her to get one. There was a note of hope, however. In the past few weeks Nick had been out to see Nell several times, and that was so far out of the ordinary that even the servants had noticed.

"Why don't I take her out alone?" Nick said.

Abbie glanced at Stan in surprise, then looked back at Nick. "Certainly, Nick. Why, that's a grand idea. It's a little chilly for us out there, anyway, I should think."

Stan winked at Nell. "You show your dad around, sweetheart. I don't believe he's seen the new barn yet."

Nell crawled off Nick's lap and looked over at her nanny, who was still standing quietly in the doorway. " 'Bye, Nanny. I'm going with him."

Nick watched the tiny child carefully. She lisped a little when she talked; he'd never noticed that before. He wondered what other things he'd never noticed. There were probably hundreds. He thought of Mickey Sullivan skipping across the fields at the Thorne Estate, and Bridget's mob of kids chattering and laughing with bright eyes, their pockets full of cookies. Did Nell chatter and laugh? Maybe when he wasn't around, which was nearly all the time, and when she was with her grandparents or her nanny.

"Ready?" He smiled down into the child's serious, dark eyes.

"Yes," she said softly, again with that hint of a lisp, and she reached with small, curled fingers for his hand.

Hours later, over a dinner served on an elegantly set table beside wide French doors, as they watched the sun set over the hills behind the house, Nick suggested to Abbie that he bring Halley for dinner the next night, rather than waiting until the weekend.

Abbie and Stan thought that was a wonderful idea, and Abbie insisted that she could call Halley herself to arrange a time.

Nick drove home with the windows open, speeding down the nearly empty highway with the moon hanging ominously above him.

Both his mind and his heart were full to the point of pain. There were so many things to sort out, to put in place, and overriding everything was the intensity of his love for Halley Finnegan and the fear that he might lose her.

How could Halley, who drew children to her like a magnet and loved them so unquestioningly, whose whole upbringing was based on dishing out love to anyone who needed it—how could she ever understand him giving up his own child for others to raise, suspending his love, living in a vacuum?

Perhaps if she had known from the beginning . . . But it hadn't been an issue then. It hadn't been relevant, not until now. Not until his life focus had shifted from mindless distraction to loving. To loving Halley. To bringing Nell back into his life.

Tomorrow. Tomorrow it would all get sorted out.

"It's important, Nick. You know that, or I wouldn't ask you to go. Your presence there will make all the difference." The older man pressed his hands on the edge of Nick's desk and leaned forward.

"I know, George." Nick sat back and ran one hand tiredly through his hair. Even Halley's voice on the telephone before he went to bed the previous night and her enthusiasm over Stan and Abbie's dinner invitation hadn't been enough to entice sleep. And the last thing he wanted to do that day was fly to Chicago to work out bank problems. Hell, he was having enough problems handling his own life.

"The meeting is first thing in the morning. We can be back here by late afternoon." George looked at him carefully. "And whatever is causing those wrinkles in your forehead, Nick, I sure hope she's worth it!"

Nick half smiled. "You can bet your fortune on it, and I guess I'd better call her to tell her our dinner date is off."

George chuckled. "Don't worry, Nick, if she's as

THE BARON • 153

terrific as that look on your face indicates, she'll be
here when you get back."

Nick nodded and reached for the phone as George
walked out of the room.

Halley hid her disappointment as best she could.
"Well, at least I know you really have a job," she said
jokingly. "There were days there when I seriously
doubted it."

"You thought I was a plastic playboy, that's it."
Just hearing her voice brought a peace back into
his life. He leaned back in the chair and pretended
Halley was standing in front of him or, better yet,
sitting on his lap, making those small wiggling
movements.

"Never plastic, my Baron, not you. A playboy? Well,
perhaps."

"Halley?" Nick's voice dropped suddenly.

"Yes?" It almost startled her, this sudden shift in
tone. His voice was thick and edged with emotion.

"I love you very much."

Halley bit down on her lip. Archie was standing
just outside the open office door fixing a broken
shade, and she was sure the sparks that shot through
her would send him in with a fire extinguisher. She
was hoping that not seeing Nick for two days might
calm the fires and replace the desire she felt for him
with a more manageable, respectable emotion, but
it hadn't worked. Her love for him was a wild, uncontrollable love. She knew now what people meant
when they talked about *lust*. Yes, she lusted after
Nick Harrington! She pressed her legs together and
spoke softly into the phone. "Nick, if you knew what
you were doing to me, you'd hang up and get over
here immediately."

"The closet?"

"Uh-huh."

"I wish I wish I could." His throat was tight.

"Me too."

Nick didn't want to hang up. It didn't matter what they said, as long as he knew she was there at the end of the phone line, as long as he could hear her breathing and feel the smile in her voice. "I'll let Abbie Melrose know we're not coming, and we'll go this weekend instead."

George knocked on the door and motioned that the cab was there to take him home to pack, and then to the airport. "Halley, I have to go."

"Don't worry about Abbie, Nick. I'll call and tell her. May the wind be at your back, my love."

She hung up and felt an insane desire to rush to the airport and surprise him, or maybe hide inside his suitcase. No, she thought, scolding herself, librarians didn't do such things. Now Rosie, *she* might do that. Halley laughed as she shuffled through some scraps of paper, looking for the Melroses' phone number. Maybe in another life she'd come back as a Rosie and have all the fun. Then her thoughts turned to Nick and she decided she'd settle for exactly what she had at this moment. For however long it lasted. She dialed the number.

Neither she nor Nick had talked about the future, or what followed after saying "I love you." And Halley hadn't pushed it. She didn't want to disturb the incredible joy Nick's love had brought her, didn't want to rock the boat . . . so she pushed all threatening thoughts away, including the nagging, relentless suspicion that although Nick had given her his love, there were still important parts of his life he hadn't begun to share with her.

A prim and proper voice on the phone announcing the Melrose residence broke into her thoughts.

Halley's voice tumbled across the line. "Hello. May I please speak to Mrs. Melrose?"

The maid announced that the Melroses were not available, but she would be pleased to take a message.

"All right, thank you," Halley said. "Please tell them

that Nick Harrington and Halley Finnegan will not be—" A sudden idea struck her and she paused in mid-sentence, reorganizing her thoughts. It was short notice to cancel out for dinner. Besides, she'd be moping around all night thinking about Nick, so she might as well be with people close to him. It might be just what she needed to put to rest those irrational suspicions about the man she loved. Furthermore, Abbie Melrose had been so warm in her invitation that Halley was certain it would be all right.

"Ma'am?"

"Oh, yes, excuse me. Would you please tell Mrs. Melrose that there will only be one of us coming for dinner tonight, rather than two as she expected? Thank you."

The drive out to the Melrose estate was beautiful at dusk. Muted shadows fell across the lovely, sculptured hills, and trees and houses were backlit by the glow of the setting sun. Halley thought of Nick the whole time, wondering if it was difficult for him to drive past these same lovely pines and giant oaks, wondering if at every turn of the curling road he thought of Anne and the times when they must have made the drive together.

She wondered and she hurt for him, but she felt no twinge of jealousy that he had loved Anne so much. It was too honest a love for her to envy.

She reached the Melrose estate just as the sky gave way to stars and moonlight, and with a feeling of anticipation she turned into the long, wooded drive.

Stan Melrose opened the door himself.

"Halley! What a nice surprise. So you made it, after all. We were told only Nick was coming, but this is wonderful."

"Oh, Stan, I'm terribly sorry. I think there was a misunderstanding." Halley's hand flew to her cheek.

Just then Abbie Melrose walked into the room, her frail body supported tonight by a slender cane she carried in one hand. "Halley, darling, hello." She kissed Halley on her cheek. "And where is our Nick?"

Abbie shook her head apologetically. "I'm terribly sorry, Abbie. There was a misunderstanding. When I called to say that only one of us was coming, I meant me. Nick had to go to Chicago and asked me to cancel. But I decided impulsively to come along alone. I hope I haven't created any problems." Her eyes moved from one to the other.

Abbie smiled kindly. "Of course not, dear! We are thrilled to see you. It will give us all a chance to get to know each other better. Come into the living room and sit."

Halley had just turned to follow Abbie's petite figure across the hall when a movement on the curved staircase caught her eye.

"Why, hello," Halley said softly, looking into the most beautiful dark eyes she had ever seen. Instinctively she walked to the stairs and got there just as the small girl reached the bottom step. Halley crouched down until her eyes were level with the child's, and smiled warmly.

"Oh, Nell." Stan turned around just then and spotted her. "We have a friend we want you to meet." He was beside them in a minute, his face beaming. "Nell, this is Miss Finnegan. Halley, this is Nell."

"Nell." Halley reached out and took one small hand in her own. "What a beautiful name you have. I'm so pleased to meet you, Nell."

The girl offered her a smile; it was tentative at first, and then she relaxed as Halley held her hand.

She was breathtaking, Halley thought. Like a portrait, with such lovely, creamy skin and those huge black eyes. Those eyes . . .

Halley watched as Nell dropped her eyes down to concentrate for a minute on the bottom step. Thick lashes swept her pink cheeks, and then they lifted, and she looked at Halley again. They were familiar, those eyes. Could Nell have visited her library at one time? Not likely, but possible. Where, then? Halley looked up and saw Abbie and Stan both watching her with an expression she couldn't quite read. She looked back at Nell. "Do you live near here, Nell?"

"I live here." Her voice was petal-soft, not boisterous or full of uncontrollable laughter like Halley's nieces and nephews.

"Here?" Halley lifted her brows and looked over the little girl's shoulder at Abbie.

Abbie's smile had faded. "Nell is our grandchild, Halley. We thought Nick had told you."

"Grandchild?" The word registered slowly. Grandchild. Those deep, familiar, smoky eyes . . . She looked at Nell. She was still holding on to Halley's hand, her head tilted slightly to one side as she watched Halley curiously.

"Grandchild," Halley whispered into the still air.

"Yes." Abbie rested one hand on Halley's shoulder. "This is Nick's daughter, Halley."

Later Halley couldn't remember walking to the living room, but she knew Nell still held her hand, because when she sat down, Nell was there beside her and carefully climbed up to sit next to her on the love seat. Halley's heart hammered wildly inside the thin wall of her chest, and she felt the sting of irrational tears building up behind her lids. She couldn't deal with it all now, not with the fact that the man she loved had neglected to tell her there was this beautiful little girl in his life. *If* she was in his life. She lived *here*, she had said. No, Halley thought, fighting the painful emotions tearing at her stomach. Don't try to piece it all together now, she told herself. Nell was sitting next to her, and she must attend to that.

"How old are you, Nell?" Halley asked quietly.

The innocent look on the little girl's face calmed Halley, and her smile was warm and sincere as she watched Nell's eyes smile back.

"I'm four."

Four. She must have been born just before Anne died, Halley thought, a huge knot forming in her throat. She finally managed to find her voice and squeezed Nell's hand gently. "I have a nephew *and* a niece who are both four. They're twins, and I think they'd love to meet you sometime."

Nell's eyes lit up. "Do they like horses?" she asked shyly.

"I'm sure they do," Halley said. She fingered the long, silky hair that fell down Nell's back. *Nick's daughter, and he never once mentioned this beautiful, vulnerable little girl.* The thought screamed at her, and she wanted to cover her ears to block out the noise.

"Can they come see me?" She looked from Halley to Abbie and Stan, then back to Halley again.

"Maybe someday. We'll see, Nell."

Abbie and Stan filled in the conversation as best they could, dropping brief explanations when they could slip them in. Abbie looked crushed, Halley thought, as if Nick had somehow deceived her as well by keeping Nell a secret from Halley. By the time dinner was served, Halley knew Nell had always lived with Abbie and Stan and that she had a nanny. Although the words were never spoken, Halley knew instinctively that Nick was a virtual stranger in this little girl's life. The thought twisted inside of her like a poisonous snake, and she sent most of her dinner back untouched.

"Miss Finn—" Nell said as she put her fork down after dessert.

"Halley. Please call me Halley." Nell hadn't left her side all evening. Halley was used to that; she loved children and they sensed it, and so they responded to her in kind. But tonight it was different. Nell's closeness was slowly causing her heart to break, and she couldn't have begun to explain it to anyone.

"Halley," Nell said with a small smile. "Will you come see my horse?"

Halley looked at Abbie and Stan and realized the pressure the evening had caused for them. Abbie looked very tired, and she had lost the color in her cheeks long before the dessert was served. Perhaps a moment alone would be good for them. She smiled at Nell and lightly touched her cheek. "I would love to see your horse, darling, but then I must leave."

She thought she saw a flash of sadness in the little girl's eyes, but it was gone quickly, replaced by the serious, polite look that she had come to expect.

A short time later she kissed Nell good-bye and waved as she climbed the winding steps to join her nanny. The Melroses seemed almost relieved, she thought, when she refused their kind offer to stay and talk. She couldn't talk just yet; she needed to be alone. So she said good-bye to them on the wide brick steps and drove off into the black night.

What she felt, when she was finally able to give proper vent to her feelings in the aloneness of her small car, was not relief, but a sorrow of such incredible dimensions that she had to pull the car over to the shoulder of the road while her tears flowed unchecked down her face.

For a long time Halley didn't try to figure out why, or for whom, she was crying. She simply allowed the horrible pain within her to flow freely. Finally, when the tears had numbed her pain, and after a truck driver stopped to see if she was in trouble, she managed to pull her car back on the road and drive home. She forced her mind to clear, but the pain remained, and when Halley finally walked into her apartment an hour later, she was emotionally exhausted.

"Halley you look like a wreck." Rosie jumped up from the couch and clicked off the television. "My Lord in heaven, what's the matter with you?"

In seconds she had wrapped her arms around the shaking body of her best friend and pulled her down beside her on the sofa.

"Rosie"—Halley's voice was quivering, and she fought the tears she knew were seconds away from spilling forth—"what are you doing here?"

"My TV is broken. I came by to watch my prime-time soaps, but I have a feeling, dear one, that you have one all your own."

"I don't mean to be rude, Ros—" Her voice broke then, and she gave in to the comfort of Rosie's arms and the shoulder that was there for her.

"Shh, you don't have to talk." Rosie held her and gently rocked her back and forth.

In bits and pieces Rosie learned about Nell, and about Nick leaving her to be raised by her aging grandparents . . . and a nanny.

"How could I have loved him, Rosie? How could I have loved someone who would desert his own daughter?"

Rosie had no answers. She and Halley had been raised the same way, with families that had a bottomless supply of love. They both had fathers who would grieve if they went more than a day or two without a call or a visit from each child. They had been nourished on hugs and laughter.

Maybe the new day would bring some solutions, Rosie suggested, and finally convinced Halley to rest for a few hours.

Rosie pulled the covers down, and Halley slid between them. "Thanks, Rosie. You're a dear friend."

Rosie smiled wanly. "If only dear friends had magic potions to make true love run smoothly."

"It can't be true love unless it's honest, Rosie."

"I don't know about that. I do know how much you love children and that this is probably the worst thing Nick could have kept from you. But, Halley, I also know that you love Nick Harrington in a way many people only dream about. It's too enormous to be dissolved in the space of an evening. It has to mean something. It has to."

Rosie looked down, and Halley's eyes were closed, but new tears fell slowly down her cheeks.

Twelve

When Halley didn't answer her phone, Nick became distraught, but a phone call from Abbie Melrose upon his return from Chicago told him everything he needed to know.

"Nicky, she didn't know you had a daughter," Abbie's tired voice had said. "How could you not have told her that?"

Because he would have had to say he deserted his daughter when she was two weeks old and went one whole year without ever seeing her; that's why, he acknowledged. Then, when he did see her, it was as if he were a stranger who'd come to visit, a man she called Daddy but had no earthly idea why. Halley's past would allow her no framework within which to understand that. The thoughts ran through his mind, but aloud he only said, "It was a dreadful mistake, Abbie. Where is Halley?"

No one seemed to know. When he called the library, she had just gone out. When he called the cottage, no one answered. When he checked with Joe Finnegan at his shop, he suggested perhaps Nick wait a few days, then try to contact her again.

• • • •

"Darlin'," Joe said, hugging Halley close, "this isn't like you to avoid the problem. You need to see Nick."

"Pop, it's not a problem. It's just over." She buried her head in his shoulder and tried to absorb the strength she felt there.

"Ah, and it's far from over, Halley. Not when you still love him so." He pulled her into his office and closed the door.

"But *who* do I love, Pop? There's a whole part of Nick he has never allowed me to see. Now he's out there in front of me, this other Nick, and I don't know who he is or what to do."

Her eyes were filled with sorrow, and Joe didn't have an answer. "All I know, little one, is that the Nick I met was not a bad person. He's a special sort. Maybe he had a few bad breaks. Maybe he even made some mistakes, but he wasn't a bad fellow. That much I know as sure as there's a God in heaven."

"Well, you're right about one thing, Pop. I need to see Nick. I've never run away from anything before, and I won't now."

"That's my girl." He hugged her briskly.

"I need to see him, talk to him, and tell him," she repeated.

"Tell him what, Halley Elizabeth?"

"I don't know, Pop. I don't know."

Halley thought Nick's office would be the best place to meet—businesslike, no memories to play games with her emotions, privacy without being private—but when she stood in the lobby of the glass-fronted bank building and faced the shiny elevator that would take her up to the executive suites, she wasn't so sure. The only thing she was sure of was that she was terrified.

"Come on, Finnegan. This is your life here. Handle it." She breathed deeply and shoved her emotions to the bottom of her soul while she tugged all her courage to the fore. She was fine until Nick's secretary ushered her into his walnut-paneled office, then her knees started to buckle beneath her.

"May I sit down?" she murmured, and slipped quickly into a chair next to his desk.

Nick sat very still in his high-backed chair, his hands flat on the tooled leather arms, his eyes filled with sadness. He fought back the desire to swallow her in his embrace, to press her to him and never let go.

Neither one of them spoke, and Halley concentrated on a narrow strip of inlaid wood that bordered the desk. Finally Nick leaned forward, his arms pressing heavily into the desk. "Halley, I'm sorry."

Halley lifted her gaze for the first time. He looked the same. Somehow she had thought maybe he would have changed because of the new knowledge she had about him. She'd convinced herself it would be all right because there'd be a stranger sitting in front of her, not the man she had so passionately loved.

But it was the same Nick—the same thick black hair into which she had dug her fingers, the same lips she had kissed, the same body that had given her such incredible joy. All that was different were his lovely black eyes, which now looked tired and worried. She took off her glasses and dropped them into her purse.

"That's the game you play with your little niece, isn't it?"

His voice matched his eyes, but Halley didn't know how to block that out. "Pardon?"

"Taking your glasses off. You know, that 'if I can't see you, you can't see me' thing that little Quinn loves."

"Oh." Halley managed a smile. Her facial muscles

felt sore and unused. "Maybe meeting here wasn't a good idea. Would you like to take a walk?"

"There's a park just across the street." Nick was out of the chair and nearly to the door when she rose to join him.

Outside, a crisp breeze scuttled clouds across a heavy, gray sky. Thunder and traffic noises filled in the stretches of silence, making Halley more comfortable. "This is much better," she said as Nick led her across the busy street and down a tree-lined path.

They walked side by side, not touching, but as aware of each other's bodies as they would be if they were naked in bed.

"Nothing's better yet, but we can make it be. I love you, Halley, and I know you still love me, somewhere beneath it all," he said matter-of-factly. "Don't you think we ought to talk about it?"

"I don't know about the love, Nick," Halley said slowly, her heart beginning to tear. "I love parts of you, but I don't know what the other parts are. I don't know if they're stronger or weaker or what kind of havoc they can build between us." When her voice traveled back on the breeze, it sounded like a bad tape recording, not at all filled with the misery she felt.

"I understand that. And I know exactly what meeting Nell must have done to you."

"She's so lovely, Nick. How . . . how could you possibly have—" Her voice broke.

Nick stuffed his hands deep into his pockets, and his shoulders lifted slightly, then fell. "I won't make excuses, Halley. I know in your eyes I did a terrible thing."

"Yes."

When he spoke again, his voice was deeper and far away as it painfully pulled things out of his past. "I was in no condition to be a parent back then. I had absolutely nothing to give an infant. No love. Nothing. I was an empty shell. She was one week old when Anne died. *One* week—" His voice grew louder, as if he were hearing it for the first time.

"So you walked away. Gave all your responsibility— your flesh and blood, for God's sake!—to a lovely couple far too old to be raising an infant."

"They provided—"

"They provided a nanny, Nick, because they *had* to!" The thread of anger rising up in her felt good. Halley thought if she could just hang on to it, she wouldn't drown. "You gave her up to the same kind of life *you* lived as a child—a series of nannies, no parent that she would ever know well. And the part she played in your life was so insignificant, you never even mentioned her to me."

Halley searched his face as she talked, and she saw the pain flash across his eyes. She desperately wanted him to come up with an answer that would make sense to her. She wanted him to tell her it all had been a dreadful mistake.

Nick walked on, his head down, his jaw clenched, his eyes on the path in front of him. The mixture of emotions was so great, he didn't trust himself to speak. The stakes were so heartbreakingly high.

Halley looked up at the sky, and a raindrop fell onto her forehead. She looked down without wiping it away. "I can understand some of it, Nick. I know it must have been difficult when Nell's mother died. For a while. What I can't understand is how you could have stayed away from her later, denying her your love." Her voice dropped until it was barely a whisper. "That's what I can't understand at all."

Nick tried to think through her words clearly but was having difficulty wading back into those muddy, murky waters. She was talking about emotions and decisions that were made by another person a lifetime ago, before her, when the world was a hellhole, stripped of meaning.

"Halley," he said, his voice rough with emotion. "I can't ask you to accept it, and I can't give you answers to make it all go away. But I beg you to give us a chance. Halley, I want to marry you—"

Halley felt her throat tighten and clog with tears. She prayed desperately that she wouldn't cry. Not now. She needed what few wits she had left to stay intact. "Nick, I can't talk sensibly to you because I don't know who you are. Do you understand that?" The tears stung viciously. "I feel like I need to start all over, figure out who you are. And I don't know if I can do that, Nick." She was crying in earnest, the tears running unchecked.

They had circled the small park and were back at the entrance across from Nick's offices.

"Back where we started from," Nick murmured. "At least that's somewhere." She turned quietly and walked back across the street.

Halley threw all her energy into the piles of library work that had accumulated since the weekend. Work, work, work, she cried silently. The panacea of the soul. But who was she fooling? No, it wasn't work at all that could help her limping soul. Damn!

She tried not to think about Nick for a while, tried to let the wounds slowly heal, and then maybe she could think more clearly. But the effort was so great, she could barely keep her head up when she and Archie returned from a cemetery storytelling session the next week.

"You look awful, Finnegan."

"Thanks, Arch."

"I mean it. And Mr. Nicholas Harrington the Third is conspicuous by his absence around here."

Halley nodded.

"I actually miss the gentleman's company."

"Me too."

"Then—?"

"We're too mismatched, Archie. Oil and water. He thinks differently."

Archie rubbed his rough beard and watched Halley with concern as she stood at the library's back door. "Oil and water can make a spicy vinaigrette, my little one."

"I don't think so, Archie. I really don't think so." She forced a smile to her face. "Don't worry, Archie, I'll get over this."

Archie looked at her out of eyes lined with the experience of life. "You do that, Finnegan, but make sure in the process that you let that Irish soul tell you a thing or two—and don't make a damn mess out of things."

Halley looked at him for a long moment, then turned and walked slowly into the library.

Thirteen

Halley was sure she'd feel better soon, or at least be able to begin picking up the pieces and glueing them back together. Finnegans were liked that, she told herself.

Each day when she woke up, she'd swear to make it a wonderful day, to transfer herself back, mind and soul, to the life that had been filled with simple joys and easy, satisfying hours, to when the most perplexing thing to mark her day was a misplaced library book or a board member vetoing a new program.

But she never made it through her second cup of morning tea before thoughts of Nick consumed her.

"Finnegan, this can't go on any longer." Rosie's words flew through the cottage door and were followed the next second by her body. "It's been two weeks now, and you look like hell."

"That seems to be a universal opinion. Would you like a cup of tea?"

Rosie shook her head and sat down at the kitchen table. "Halley, somehow you have to work this out."

"I know." Her voice was barely audible. Sleepless

nights nourished little energy, she'd discovered quickly.

"Do you love him?"

"Yes." It was useless to say she didn't; Rosie would know, anyway, no matter what she said. "It's a curse, Rosie."

"Love is a curse?"

"Yes. No. I don't know!" She leaned her elbows on the table and cupped her head in her hands. "Oh, hell, Rosie, I don't know. I can't live without Nick. I'm going crazy, but I couldn't marry him, Rosie. Not now."

Rosie was silent.

"I don't think I could. I think of loving him forever, and then I see Nell in my mind, this precious little girl, and Nick's face changes. He becomes someone I don't know, someone who could put his own daughter on a shelf—"

"Halley, that's harsh—"

She shook her head and wiped away the buildup of tears that had clouded her eyes. "I know. See, Rosie? See what all this is doing to me? I'm not a harsh person, dammit!"

"Maybe if you opened yourself a little more, Halley," Rosie said very quietly.

"To what, Rosie? I've opened myself so wide, I feel like I'm split in two."

"Open yourself to understanding what the hell it must have been like for Nick Harrington four years ago."

"I try to do that. And I can get all the way up to spending the rest of my life with him. Then I get scared."

Halley's voice was so sad that Rosie's eyes filled with tears. "I know, Finnegan. Sometimes life's a big, scary bitch. Remember when we were kids and used to imagine the ghosts of the Indians out in the Thorne cemetery?"

Halley managed a small smile. "I remember. At first we were frightened witless."

"And when we became friends with Small Owl and Blue Feathers and Whisper Cloud, all the fear left."

Halley nodded, remembering the games they'd played with their ghostly friends, the food they left for them behind the bushes, and the endless stories she and Rosie wove about the Indian children. "If only this were that easy, Rosie," she said, half to herself. "If only Nick Harrington were a ghost. . . ."

Nights were the hardest. Halley would curl up in her bed and try to block out thought. She'd gone from counting sheep, to graves in the cemetery, to books in the reference section of the library. Nothing helped.

"Oh, Nick, will you ever leave me in peace?" she cried into the damp pillow one moonless night. Then she remembered something. Slowly she crawled out of bed in the dark, and with her fingers she found the warm-ups she had borrowed from him that very first night together. She slipped out of her nightgown and pulled the sweatshirt over her head, then tugged on the large, baggy pants until her naked body was completely wrapped in Nick's clothes. When she crawled back into bed, the lovely, musky smell of intimacy, of Nick floated around her until finally she drifted off to sleep, filled with dreams of Nick cradling her aching body.

The next Saturday's errands went by the wayside. Even the Green Knight didn't get its weekly checkup.

It was a beautiful fall day when Halley slipped behind the wheel of her car, determined to make the day worthwhile—somehow.

It hadn't been planned, but she felt good when

she realized she was on the highway heading toward Abbie and Stan Melroses'—and to Nell.

In between thoughts of Nick, Nell had been very much on her mind. She would just stop to say hello, see how the horses were.

"Halley, you are a most welcome sight, my dear." Abbie Melrose sat still on the couch, but her eyes told Halley everything. They knew the whole story.

"Have you seen Nick?" Halley asked softly.

"Every day, dear, for the past two weeks. More than we have seen of Nicky for one stretch since he was married to Anne." Her clear eyes never left Halley's face. She was telling her so much and wanted Halley to hear it.

"He's come to see Nell." Halley looked down and let the words sink in.

"Please sit here next to me, Halley. There are some things perhaps Nick hasn't told you, but first I need to know one thing, although I think I know the answer. Do you love him?"

"Oh, Abbie." Halley felt the tears build up behind her lids. "I love Nick more than I dreamed possible."

"Good, dear. That's what I wanted to hear. And he loves you so very much." Abbie's hands folded and unfolded in her lap, as if her fingers would help her pick out just the right words. She began slowly. "Halley, Nick and our daughter were very much in love."

Halley nodded slowly.

"And they lived a blissful three years before Anne got pregnant. It was a wonderful time for Nick. He had never had anyone in his life before who really cared for him." She stopped, as if she had said something unfair. "I don't mean to say that the Harringtons were bad people; they weren't. They were lovely. But they never wanted children. Nick was a mistake, and everyone knew that."

Halley cringed. Nick was not a mistake. He was a wonderful, caring man—

"They would never have abandoned him to someone else, of course. They did all the right things, sent him to the right schools, hired the right help, but he was a stranger to them. He was always a smart child, and his looks, his intelligence, and his stubbornness got him through it all, but until he and Anne fell in love, he didn't know what it meant to be loved for himself, or to be cherished."

Halley leaned forward on the couch. The tears were still there just behind her lids, but she ignored them. She wanted to listen completely to what Abbie Melrose had to say.

"Would you like some tea?"

Halley shook her head.

"All right, then." She patted Halley's knee and continued slowly. "Anne's death was devastating to Nick. He fell apart. We convinced him to go off for a while, on his own, where he could put himself back together, and we took Nell. I don't think Nick even realized for a long time there *was* a Nell. He wasn't himself, Halley—" Abbie's thin brows drew together as she concentrated carefully on her words. "Halley, dear, it's so difficult to explain to you, but even though Nick was a strong, virile young man, the strength of Anne's love was gone, at least physically, and he had to learn how to function alone. It was very, very hard for him."

"But Anne's love was there—right there in Nell. How could he not see that and cherish it?"

Abbie nodded slowly. "Because, Halley, he didn't know how. He'd lost his framework—Anne. He had to build another one. He didn't trust himself with Nell; he felt so empty, he thought there was nothing left there to give her. And rather than do what his parents did and give her space in an empty house, he left her with us. It wasn't the perfect choice, of course. Stan and I are too old, and we had to resort to nannies to help with the child, but we have loved Nell, and we have prayed daily that her father would come back to her—"

Halley looked up as Abbie's clear voice broke. There were tears streaming down her face.

"Oh, Abbie, I'm sorry. I know how hard this is for you too."

Abbie shook her gray head and dabbed at her eyes. "No, wait, Halley, let me finish. Our prayers have been answered. We saw new life in Nick when he met you, and our hopes soared. When you broke things off, we were so frightened. We thought the same thing would happen all over again. But you've given Nick a very precious gift, Halley, and he has stubbornly refused to let go of it, thank God."

Halley wiped her eyes and looked over at Abbie. "I don't understand."

"Nick is in terrible pain. He loves you so deeply. You've shown him he can love again. His days with you have given him tremendous joy, and he won't give that up, nor what those days have taught him. He's taking Nell, Halley."

Halley's tears fell freely now.

"We don't know when. So many things have to be worked out. But Nicky has been here every night— looking awfully depressed, by the way—but he's determined not to lose what you have given him. He's opened his heart to Nell, and they are slowly getting to know each other." Abbie blew her nose delicately on a lacy hanky. "Thank you, Halley."

Halley wrapped her arms around Abbie's frail shoulders. "Oh, Abbie, I've been so selfish."

"No. You haven't understood, that's all. You had nothing—no experiences—to help you understand, just as Nicky had no experiences to help him understand how to fit Nell into his life. Now he does—because of you, dear."

"Hello, Grandma and Halley." The soft, careful voice came from the doorway, and Halley and Abbie pulled apart to look at Nell, watching them with large, luminous eyes.

They wiped their eyes quickly.

"Oh, Nell, hello!" Halley's eyes sparkled at the sight of the little girl, and for the moment she forgot her tiredness and pain.

Halley looked at Nell through the damp sheen caused by her tears. She looked different today. There was a pink blush to her cheeks and a soft light in her dark eyes that Halley hadn't noticed before.

"May I give you a hug?" Halley asked.

Nell crossed the room quickly and was smiling when she wrapped her small arms around Halley's waist.

"Nell, how is Daffodil doing?"

Nell's eyes lit up as she told Halley how Daffodil had chewed the cuffs off the stable boy's jeans.

Halley laughed and felt the stiffness in her face melting away beneath the magic of the little girl's gentle laugh. It was like a wind chime, delicate and musical.

Halley looked over Nell's shoulder at Abbie, whose eyes hadn't left the two of them. "Abbie, do you suppose Nell and I might take a walk? It's a gorgeous day out there."

"Certainly you may. Nell would like that. Nanny usually takes her out in the afternoon while I'm resting. This will be a treat."

Halley felt the excitement in the little girl's quick step, and her heart swelled. Perhaps she was dreaming, but Nick's presence in Nell's life already seemed to be affecting the child. The thought of him brought the tears back. She'd been so unfair, so narrow-minded. Would he be able to forgive her?

Outside, a fall breeze tugged leaves gently off tree branches and danced them to the ground. "Where would you like to go, Nell?" She took her hand, and their fingers twined together.

"To see the ducks?" Nell looked up at her hopefully, and Halley suspected feeding the ducks was something she only did when she could fool Nanny into traipsing all the way out to the pond.

"Sure, let's go, sweetie."

Nell skipped alongside her, and Halley watched as the wind caught her black hair and whipped it softly against her cheeks.

Nick's beautiful little girl. Nick, her Baron. She felt the swelling again; the choking, wonderful sensation that was slowly easing the pain in her heart.

"Look, Halley, flowers!" The little girl let go of Halley's hand and flew across the field toward a small collection of brilliantly colored flowers.

"Purple wildflowers are my very favorite!" Halley said. She laughed as Nell plucked one off and made Halley bend over so she could stick it in her hair.

"Now one for you, princess," she said, and wound a stem through Nell's thick black hair.

"That's what Daddy calls me," she said matter-of-factly, and skipped on to a small wooded area.

The pond was just beyond the woods, a small marshy area that was home to a flock of wild geese and seven ducks that seemed to welcome the intruders with curious quacks.

"Oh"—Nell's small face fell—"we forgot the bread."

Halley rummaged around in her purse. "Aha! We're in luck, Nell." She pulled out two slightly squashed candy bars.

Nell squealed delightedly and quickly unwrapped one, squeezing the wrapper back into Halley's hand. She carefully picked her way as close as she could get to the edge of the pond and threw out a piece of the candy.

Halley watched the laughter on Nell's face and thought about how much joy the simple act was giving her. As Halley sank down into the tall grasses beside the pond, she thought of all the other simple joys of childhood and tried to picture Nell at a birthday party playing duck-duck-goose or learning to ride a bike. Suddenly the most important thing in the world to Halley was making sure she was there to see Nell's face as she visited Santa Claus at Wanamaker's at Christmastime.

Halley felt light-headed as she imagined Nell talking to the kindly Santa, her face bright with a smile as they'd ride the train around the Christmas displays and wave to the giant stuffed animals. Then they'd go to Haverford's for hot chocolate with mounds of whipped cream on top and go ice skating in the park while the moon climbed high into the sky.

They would . . . She bit down hard on her bottom lip to stop the quivering.

"Halley, come see," Nell called to her, and Halley slipped out of the dreamy, shaky future and looked at the little girl, crouched down at the edge of the pond. One of the ducks had crawled up beside her and was nuzzling into her pocket for more candy. Nell was giggling fiercely.

"Oh, Nell." Halley laughed as she wiped away another tear and hurried to her side. "You've a friend for life, I think."

"Daisy," the little girl whispered so she wouldn't scare him away. "I named him Daisy."

Halley nodded in agreement and started to kneel down beside her. "A perfect na—"

She hadn't seen the soft, oozing mud, nor had she expected it. In a split second her tennis shoes flew out from beneath her and Halley landed with a squishy thud at the edge of the pond. The wind was knocked clear out of her for a brief moment, and she couldn't speak.

"Halley!" Nell screamed. The duck darted for the swamp, but not before he'd crashed into Nell's short, slender legs and sent her sprawling to the ground next to Halley. With a splash that cascaded up onto the ground and sprayed Nell and Halley from head to foot, he disappeared beneath the water.

"Nell, are you all right?" Halley quickly wrapped an arm around Nell's shoulders and checked her over.

"You look funny," Nell managed as a wide grin spread across her face.

Halley looked down. Her jeans and sweater were covered from head to toe with mud, and she could feel the wet drops of mud across her cheeks.

"You look pretty funny, too, my little friend." She grinned at Nell and pointed to her pink slacks.

Nell looked down and giggled. They were patterned with a fine spray of mud. Then she impulsively dug her hands into the mud and watched it squish out between her fingers.

Halley laughed as little plops landed between them. With a finger she traced a smiling face in the mud, and Nell jubilantly added eyes and ears, and their building laughter blossomed up around them.

When Nick finally found them, the backs of their heads were all he could see: Nell's long, straight black hair moving softly in the wind, and Halley's russet mane a startling contrast as it swayed with their laughter. Their legs were stuck straight out in front of them on the edge of the pond, and they appeared to be making mud pies.

The only sounds in the world were their laughter mingling with the wind and the slow, lapping movement of the water.

His heart leaped up into his throat and lodged there tightly.

Abbie had told him Halley was on the estate some-where with Nell, and then she had urged him to go and find them.

It was Nell's laughter, so pure and musical, that had led him out to the pond.

As he watched, Halley reached over and brushed Nell's hair back from her face, and he spotted the mud specks mixing with her freckles. Nell's face matched Halley's, with little streaks of dirt across her chin and cheeks.

They were beautiful.

He didn't want to speak, didn't want to let the moment move on. Could love make one explode? he wondered vaguely. He loved Halley so very, very much. His heart swelled painfully as he watched her head move back in laughter and Nell's tiny hand reach for hers. It was too big, this love, too powerful for Halley not to feel it.

Somehow she'd have to see that. Somehow . . . he took one step closer and shoved his hands deep into the pockets of his slacks.

"Hi."

Nell and Halley responded together, their heads turning to the side, then twisting back. They saw him at exactly the same moment.

Nick felt an uncomfortable sting behind his eyelids.

"Nick!"

"Daddy."

Halley's heart began to beat rapidly, and she looked to Nell to help her up. Nell laughingly tugged at her arm until the two had regained their footing.

Words collided inside her head—how she loved him, how sorry she was, how unfair she'd been. Nothing could get beyond the huge lump swelling in her throat.

Halley ran to him, her hair flying, speckles of mud scattering in the air. She threw her arms around him and held him close, her head buried in his chest and the tears rolling down onto his sweater.

It took a brief, disbelieving second for Nick to understand, and then his arms were around her tightly. "My darling . . ." he murmured into her hair.

Nell stood apart, her face bathed in smiles.

Finally, without a word, they pulled apart and looked up into each other's faces.

"Daddy," Nell said softly, "this is my friend Halley."

Nick reached out a hand and pulled Nell to them. "I could tell you were friends. Your mud matches." His voice was choked and strained, but Nell didn't seem to notice.

"Would you like to play with us?" Nell asked.

Nick looked from Nell to Halley's tear-streaked face, then back to Nell. "How about a lifetime, princess, if Halley's willing?"

Nell giggled. "Okay, but we need to go back for lunch now." She looked curiously from one adult to the other, as if she wasn't at all sure why they looked so peculiar.

She started to skip off ahead of them, and Nick and Halley followed slowly, their fingers wound tightly together. "I love you so much, Halley Elizabeth Mary Finnegan."

Halley didn't want to talk, her heart was so full, but there were things that needed to be said. "Nick, I've been so unfair to you—"

"Halley, Archie says it's irrelevant to talk about what's fair and not fair. It's a waste of time."

"Oh, he does?" She slipped her fingers loose and wrapped her arms around his waist.

"Yes, and he also said you're a wonderful person, but if you continue on this collision course with disaster, he's going to have to step in."

"I see." Her fingers played with the skin at his side, and she felt the warmth building up and encompassing her. Soon, she was sure, all breathing would stop.

"And—" Nick said huskily.

"Shh." Halley pressed her fingers to his lips.

"Ah, the Contessa wants to speak?"

"No, mostly the Contessa wants to love you. And so does Halley Finnegan. Forever." She placed one palm flat on his chest and looked up into deep black eyes that could see right down into the center of her soul.

"That's a long time," Nick murmured into her hair.

"Not nearly long enough, my Baron. Not nearly long enough."

THE EDITOR'S CORNER

The Birth of the Delaney Dynasty
Travel back to the origins
of the dynasty . . .

Iris Johansen sets the historical stage
with the enthralling

THIS FIERCE SPLENDOR

ON SALE NEXT MONTH

February is a favorite LOVESWEPT month. After all, it's the month dedicated to love and romance—and that's what we're all about! Romance is (and should be!) more important in our lives than just one special day, so LOVESWEPT is claiming February as a whole month dedicated to love. What a wonderful world it would be if we could convince everyone!

In this special month, we have six marvelous books with very pretty covers. In our LOVESWEPT Valentine month we have given all of our books covers in pink/red/purple shades—from pale pink confection, to hot fuschia pink, to red-hot-red, and passionate purple. This is our way of celebrating the month—so be sure to look for the SHADES OF LOVESWEPT covers, and we know you'll enjoy all the stories inside.

Our first book for the month, **STIFF COMPETITION**, LOVESWEPT #234, by Doris Parmett, is a heart-warming and very funny story about next door neighbors who are determined not to fall in love! Both Stacy and Kipp have been burned before and they go to ridiculous lengths to maintain their single status! But he can't resist the adorable vixen next door and she can't stop thinking of the devil-may-care hero of her dreams. When Kipp finally takes her in his arms, their resistance is swept away by sizzling passion and feel-

(continued)

ings telling them both that it's safe to trust again.

TOO HOT TO HANDLE, LOVESWEPT #235—This title tells all! Sandra Chastain's new book is full of sexy flirting, outrageous propositions, and hot pursuit. Matt Holland is a man after Callie Carmichael's classic convertible—or is it her cuddly, freckled body? Callie's not interested in any city slickers like Matt because she's a country girl living a free and easy life. But his kisses are too wonderful and they are bound to change her mind . . . and her lifestyle!

Next we have **SHARING SECRETS,** LOVESWEPT #236, by Barbara Boswell. We first met Rad Ramsey and Erin Brady in an earlier Barbara Boswell book, **PLAYING HARD TO GET,** which was a story about their siblings. Now Barbara has decided that Rad and Erin deserve a book of their own—and we agree! Sexy heartbreaker Rad knew women found him irresistible, but he'd always enjoyed the chase too much to keep the ladies whose hearts he captured. Erin had never known the fiery thrill of seduction, but Rad's touch awakened a woman who would be satisfied with nothing less. When they found each other, Rad knew he couldn't ignore his feelings and Erin knew she wanted this powerful, sensual, and loving man. This is a provocative story of a woman's first real passion and a man's true love.

Those incredible men surrounding Josh Logan are just fascinating, aren't they? Kay Hooper gives us another of the wonderful romances in what Carolyn Nichols calls the "Hagan Strikes Again Series" next month with **UNMASKING KELSEY,** LOVESWEPT #237. There is a terrible aura of fear hanging over the sleepy little town of Pinnacle, and beautiful Elizabeth Conner figures prominently in an episode that brings Kelsey there on the run and brings danger to a boil. Elizabeth also figures prominently in Kelsey's every thought, every dream . . . and she finds him utterly irresistible. This is one of Kay's most gripping and sensual romances and it seems to have "Don't You Dare Miss Me!" stamped all over it!

There's no more appealing Valentine story than
(continued)

MIDSUMMER SORCERY by Joan Elliott Pickart, Loveswept #238, an unforgettable story of first love—renewed. Fletcher McGill was back in town after six years and Nancy Forest was still furious at the man who captured her heart and then deserted her. They've been lonely difficult years and now Nancy is determined that Fletcher feel the full force of her hot anger—but instead, desire still flamed in her. Fletcher's touch scorched her, branded her with the heat that time and distance had never cooled. This time was his love as real and lasting as his passion?

We end the month with **THE PRINCE AND THE PATRIOT**, LOVESWEPT #239, a terrific book from Kathleen Creighton, a favorite LOVESWEPT author. This Valentine features a prince, some crown jewels, a European dynasty and a wonderful happy-ever-after ending. Our heroine, Willa Caris, is not a princess but a patriot. She's committed to protect the crown jewels of Brasovia, the small European country that was her parents' birthplace. Nicholas Francia is a prince in hiding and Willa doesn't know the truth behind his playboy facade. Carried away by tempestuous desire, Nicholas and Willa surrender to their intense attraction and need for one another . . . believing that the goals in their "real" lives are at odds. When the surprising truth is revealed, their love for each other proves to be as strong as their love for their traditions.

Remember to look for the six Valentine covers and spend the month in love—with LOVESWEPT!

Sincerely,

Kate Hartson

Kate Hartson
  Editor
LOVESWEPT
Bantam Books, Inc.
666 Fifth Avenue
New York, NY 10103

The first Delaney trilogy

Heirs to a great dynasty, the Delaney brothers were united by blood, united by devotion to their rugged land . . . and known far and wide as

THE SHAMROCK TRINITY

Bantam's bestselling LOVESWEPT romance line built its reputation on quality and innovation. Now, a remarkable and unique event in romance publishing comes from the same source: THE SHAMROCK TRINITY, three daringly original novels written by three of the most successful women's romance writers today. Kay Hooper, Iris Johansen, and Fayrene Preston have created a trio of books that are dynamite love stories bursting with strong, fascinating male and female characters, deeply sensual love scenes, the humor for which LOVESWEPT is famous, and a deliciously fresh approach to romance writing.

THE SHAMROCK TRINITY—Burke, York, and Rafe: Powerful men . . . rakes and charmers . . . they needed only love to make their lives complete.

☐ *RAFE, THE MAVERICK by Kay Hooper*

Rafe Delaney was a heartbreaker whose ebony eyes held laughing devils and whose lilting voice could charm any lady—or any horse—until a stallion named Diablo left him in the dust. It took Maggie O'Riley to work her magic on the impossible horse . . . and on his bold owner. Maggie's grace and strength made Rafe yearn to share the raw beauty of his land with her, to teach her the exquisite pleasure of yielding to the heat inside her. Maggie was stirred by Rafe's passion, but would his reputation and her ambition keep their kindred spirits apart?   (21846 • $2.75)

LOVESWEPT

☐ *YORK, THE RENEGADE by Iris Johansen*

Some men were made to fight dragons, Sierra Smith thought when she first met York Delaney. The rebel brother had roamed the world for years before calling the rough mining town of Hell's Bluff home. Now, the spirited young woman who'd penetrated this renegade's paradise had awakened a savage and tender possessiveness in York: something he never expected to find in himself. Sierra had known loneliness and isolation too—enough to realize that York's restlessness had only to do with finding a place to belong. Could she convince him that love was such a place, that the refuge he'd always sought was in her arms?

(21847 • $2.75)

☐ *BURKE, THE KINGPIN by Fayrene Preston*

Cara Winston appeared as a fantasy, racing on horseback to catch the day's last light—her silver hair glistening, her dress the color of the Arizona sunset . . . and Burke Delaney wanted her. She was on his horse, on his land: she would have to belong to him too. But Cara was quicksilver, impossible to hold, a wild creature whose scent was midnight flowers and sweet grass. Burke had always taken what he wanted, by willing it or fighting for it; Cara cherished her freedom and refused to believe his love would last. Could he make her see he'd captured her to have and hold forever?

(21848 • $2.75)

The Delaney Dynasty Lives On!

The Bestselling Creators Of The Shamrock Trinity Bring You Three More Sizzling Novels

The Delaneys of Killaroo

Daring women, dreamers, and doers, they would risk anything for the land they loved and the men who possessed their hearts.

☐ 26870 **ADELAIDE, THE ENCHANTRESS** $2.75

☐ 26869 **MATILDA, THE ADVENTURESS** $2.75

☐ 26871 **SYDNEY, THE TEMPTRESS** $2.75